"There's someone out there!" Julia whispered.

She moved quickly toward the night-darkened library window. When she was halfway there, a heavy foot came down on the hem of her dressing gown, and in a moment she found herself sprawled on the floor, Lord Rossiter on top of her.

"You tripped me!" she accused.

"How clumsy of me." The baron rolled away, then calmly flicked a bit of dust from his sleeve.

"Why didn't you want me to see who was out there?" Julia asked, pushing back the fall of lace from her nightcap.

"What the devil?" Rossiter grasped her chin and tilted her face to the light of the fire. Touching the discolouration beneath her eye, he demanded, "How did you come by this?"

"I...I stumbled and fell while walking in the garden," she murmured.

He didn't believe her, she knew. But she couldn't possibly tell him the truth...!

Dear Reader:

Welcome! We're glad you joined us for our new line, Harlequin Regency Romance. Two titles a month, every month, for your reading pleasure.

We know Regency readers want to be entertained, charmed and transported to that special time of magic and mischief. And we know you also like variety, so we've included everything from the Regency romp to the dramatic and touching love stories that Harlequin is famous for. We offer you authors you know and love, as well as new authors to discover and delight in. We feel we have captured the Regency spirit and are proud and pleased to share it with you.

Harlequin Regency Romance was created with you, the reader, in mind, and we'd like nothing better than to know what you think. If there's something special you would like to see included, drop us a line. If there's any way we can improve, we'd like you to tell us. We welcome your feedback and promise to consider it carefully. After all, you are our biggest fan.

We hope you enjoy reading Harlequin Regency Romance as much as we enjoyed putting it all together. And, in the true tradition of the Regency period, "we wish you happy" and look forward to hearing from you.

Marmie Charndoff
Editor

MIDSUMMER MASQUE
CORAL HOYLE

Harlequin Books

TORONTO • NEW YORK • LONDON
AMSTERDAM • PARIS • SYDNEY • HAMBURG
STOCKHOLM • ATHENS • TOKYO • MILAN

To my sisters—
Jacquie, Enid and GayLynne—
for memories of the past
and the hopes and dreams of the future.

Author's Note

Although the office of the Bishop of Bath and
Wells is an actual appointment of the Church of
England, Emory Witton did not hold the postion
in 1811. He is a fictional character, as are the
other characters in this work.

Published June 1989

ISBN 0-373-31104-4

CHAPTER ONE

THE THREE-QUARTER MOON was nearing the end of its journey across the Somerset countryside. Miss Julia Witton tapped her foot to mark the passing of each second. Then she stamped the ground and began to pace again. Would he never come? Uncertainty gripped her as she looked along the road that led from Bath. In the hazy moonlight, the dim shadows formed by the thick foliage of the trees made it difficult to see, and no sound broke the stillness to tell her of his coming.

She waited. Into the peace of the early morning came the rattle of an approaching carriage and the pounding hoofbeats of a harnessed team. The driver cracked his whip in the air, as the horses lunged forward.

Instead of stopping, as she expected, the coach sped along the road into town. But as it passed, something was hurled from it, and Julia's head became the mark for the projectile. She was struck with such force that she was knocked off her feet.

"What the devil!" She clapped a hand over her mouth and looked to the heavens with a guilty expression. "Pardon," she murmured.

She pushed herself up into a sitting position and adjusted her black toque. Touching the tingling flesh around her eye, she groped about on the ground for the source of her irritation. Her hand brushed over a wad of cloth.

Julia looked at the bundle and wondered. For something one would suppose to be soft it had struck her quite sharply. Her curiosity compelled her to pull the bundle onto her lap and investigate what was wrapped in it. She found the length of cloth to be a scarf. Lying in the middle of the scarf was a large, flat leather pouch held together with a braided, silken cord. If there were any marks of identification on the pouch she couldn't see them, not with the clouds beginning to obscure the moon. She ran her long fingers over the fine leather, wondering if the owner would return for it.

This is a most curious night, she thought. First, rather than slowing to a stop, the carriage for which she had waited half the night had gone by as if chased by demons. And if that weren't bad enough, she could feel a puffiness beginning to swell around her eye. Nothing was going as it ought.

Brushing the dust from her carriage dress as she got to her feet, she decided that she'd had enough for one night. He had not come. Three hours was quite long enough to wait. The only course left to her now was to return home.

"Blast!" Julia kicked the dirt with the toe of her half boot. Now that Harry had failed to show, her future looked black indeed.

The thunder of fast-approaching horses drew her attention. She again stationed herself by the oak tree. Her dark grey gown blended with the shadows. As the pair of riders galloped by, they failed to notice her presence.

She wondered why so many travellers were about at such an ungodly hour. Surely Harry could have made a greater effort to be among their number.

Julia took the scarf and pouch and moved to a portmanteau tucked behind the oak. Before lifting the large travelling bag, she looked once more at the end of the road and listened. Only the quiet sounds of the night came to her ears. She proceeded to trudge the short distance to a footpath known as Lovers' Walk. Despite her troubles her thoughts went to the leather packet she carried. Why would someone throw such a thing out of a coach window? And who could it have been?

IN THE TRUNK-LADEN posting chaise that sped along the road, a young lady sat clutching her breast and glaring at her companion. "What have you done! We dare not stop lest we be caught." The young lady moaned. "How could you be so witless? Throwing it out the window like that! Now Philippe never will forgive me!"

Marie, the young lady's French maid, winced at the shrill sound of her mistress's voice. "You can tell him where to find the pouch when he comes to seek you out." Marie clutched at her shawl. "You said that you must not be caught with the papers. So...I marked the spot by the large oak and threw the bundle. Simple!"

The lady screeched with frustration and burst into tears. "I have failed my dearest heart! Will he ever forgive me?"

"*Madam's* husband? He would forgive you anything. He loves you."

"My husband! I wasn't speaking of him, you fool."

The coach began to slow and the wheels jarred over cobblestones.

The lady leaned out of the carriage window and shouted to the post boy, "Where are we?"

The fellow riding the near horse looked up at the dark shadows of a cathedral. "Wells, ma'am."

"Hurry! Do not let them catch us." The young lady fell back upon the seat. "He'll kill me. I know it."

"That Philippe, he may slap you a little, but he won't kill you, not yet," said Marie. "Not until he has his hands on those papers."

Pulling up short in her flight of dramatics, the lady cast the maid a scathing glance. "I was not speaking of Philippe, but of that son of Satan who's following us. If my stepbrother catches me, he will wring my neck." She paused, her blue eyes widening with fear. "Do you hear riders approaching?" Without waiting for an answer, she again thrust her head out into the night air. "It's he!" She fell back once again with a moan.

"How can you be sure, Madam Fitzsimmons? In the moonlight all riders look the same."

The lady gave the maid a disdainful glare. "No one rides like he does. He is a devil on horseback. Oh, why did I do it!"

"That Philippe, he would have killed you if you refused."

"Kill me! Never! He loves me as I love him. Our love is pure. I am sure he would have been quite...quite vexed if I had not done as he asked of me. The cause means so much to him." The lady sighed. "You do not understand his finer feelings, Marie. He told me that I was the only one who truly understood him." She dabbed at her eyes as she recalled that touching scene. "If only my devil of a stepbrother would leave us in peace, all would be well."

"*Madam*, you would speak so of his lordship?"

"Mind your tongue! I shall speak as I wish. My stepbrother is a beast!"

The maid peered out the window. "I fear the beast is about to take us in his jaws."

The two riders pursuing the carriage were scarcely fifty yards behind the posting chaise. They spurred their mounts, holding to the road in the dim moonlight.

The post boy seemed to disregard the condition of the road as he whipped the horses to greater speed. Even as the road began to curve sharply he kept up the breakneck pace.

"Faster, I say. Faster!" the lady ordered the postillion. "Make them go faster!"

"Can't! The nags are spent," he shouted back. "We've got to stop soon."

Drawing her head into the coach and sitting back against the dusty squabs, the lady straightened the hood of her cloak over the dark curls that framed her pretty face. Her hand trembled as she did so.

"Is he still after us?" asked Marie.

"I daresay he is. My stepbrother never gives up once he wants something." She clasped her hands together. "Oh, Marie, I never should have done it! But my love for Philippe is too great. What could I do?"

The maid sat expressionless before her mistress. "It is wisest to do what that one asks of you, *n'est-ce pas*? To refuse Philippe would have brought you great pain." She rubbed her cheek and looked away.

"Foolish girl! Why must you always utter such nonsense? My Philippe is good. He loves me. He loves *me*! Oh, my darling Philippe, where are you when I need you so desperately?" She buried her head in her hands and wept prettily.

On the outskirts of Glastonbury, on the road from Wells, the post boy guided the horses into the yard of the Angel Inn. He shouted for service and soon raised the innkeeper from his bed.

Inside the chaise the lady continued to cry. As her sobs built to a crescendo, the carriage door was jerked open. She stopped in midwail and stared.

Catching the light from the coach lamps, something silver flashed on the face of the man who stood before her. The lady gasped.

"Damn you, Trixie! Where is it?" he demanded in an icy voice.

CHAPTER TWO

As SHE WALKED toward the large Palladian manor house, carrying her portmanteau and the pouch, Julia was cheered by the darkened windows. The manor house lay in a state of majestic peacefulness. No one was waiting for her.

She let herself in by a long window, one of many that opened to the back terrace, and stealthily made her way through the main drawing room to the hall. At the stairs she paused to put the pouch into her bag, then hoisted up the skirt of her gown. She did not want to trip on the hem as she climbed the stairs—her mother tended to wake at the least sound. With portmanteau in hand, she crept up the stairs, testing each step as she went.

It was ridiculous for a lady of four-and-twenty summers to be creeping about in her family home like a thief. But her father was a stern man, and the deportment of his daughter was of no little concern to him. He would give a high sermon if he caught one of his girls sneaking into the house a few hours before dawn. If he knew the reason for Julia's behaviour he would have apoplexy before banishing her forever.

At the landing, where the stairs branched up to the east and west wings of the house, she stopped to catch her breath. If Harry had come, she thought, then all this creeping about would not be necessary. Foxed. He was undoubtedly foxed. But even drunk as a wheel about to slip its pin he could drive to an inch. There was no reason for his defection other than a change of heart. How humiliating!

A sting of tears plagued her eyes as she made her way to the east wing of the house. The door to the young ladies' bedchamber opened quietly at her touch. The large room held four beds in addition to the various pieces of furniture that the daughters of the house needed. By the clouded moonlight, Julia saw the sleeping forms of her younger sisters. She moved toward her bed, then stopped short. There was someone sleeping in it!

The lump in the bed turned over. The edging of a nightcap peeked out just above the bedclothes. Julia heaved a sigh of relief. She set her bag down and tiptoed to the bedside.

"Sarah," she whispered, as she gave her youngest sister's shoulder a shake.

"Huh?" Sarah rolled over and continued to sleep.

Julia shook the girl again. "Wake up," she said in distinct tones near the fourteen-year-old's ear.

A few groans and moans came from the depths of the bed. Sarah's head emerged from under the covers. "Julia! I don't know where she—" Sarah rubbed her eyes and gaped at her sister. "What are you doing here?"

"You snatched the words from my mouth. What are you doing in my bed?"

"When you left to meet Harry, I thought I'd create a diversion for you." She yawned. "I put an old quilt in my bed and got in yours so you wouldn't be found out. Where's Harry? Why did you come back?"

Julia smoothed her light brown hair back as she removed her hat and gloves. "Harry...Harry failed to meet me."

"What!"

"Shhh," Julia whispered.

"That malingerer! He must be disguised with blue ruin."

Julia tried not to smile. "Sarah Witton," she said, using the deep tones of her sire, "what would Father say if he heard you speaking cant phrases?"

"We'll never know, for I'm not mutton-headed enough to let him catch me at it. Oh, I could box Harry's ears. Now what will you do?"

"I daresay I'll have to go through with what Mother and Father want."

"Don't do it. You would be miserable."

"I know." Julia looked down at her hands. When it appeared that her emotions would overcome her, she gathered her forces and smiled in her engaging way. "How did you know about tonight?"

"I listened when you met Harry in the garden last night. I knew something was in the wind the moment I saw him creep onto the grounds from Lovers' Walk." Sarah beamed proudly. "Did you know, one can see everything from up here. That's the only good thing about being sent to bed early. Much more happens during the night than during the day. Why, the kitchen maid and the undergroom—"

"Sarah! 'Tis hardly ladylike to spy on people, especially the servants."

"Yes, but then you cannot know what they were doing!"

Julia held up her hand, then grinned. "Do you think you are the only one to, ah, star gaze when sent to bed early?" She tugged the front of Sarah's nightcap down a bit. "Thank you for wanting to help, but if Father had caught you at it you would be reading tomes on decorum for a week. Now, off to your own bed." She turned to help Sarah out from under the bedclothes.

"What happened to your eye?" the girl asked in a fierce whisper. "Let me light a candle and see."

"No. Just go back to sleep." Pushing Sarah out of the bed, Julia sat down to examine her eye. She winced. It only needed that to make the night a thorough disaster.

Sarah touched Julia's shoulder. "Well, you *almost* had an adventure." She yawned. "Good night."

Taking off her dark grey pelisse, Julia began to unpack the portmanteau. She looked down at the pouch. It seemed to beckon to her. Well, she reasoned, if one is to discover the identity of the owner one must examine the contents.

She glanced over at Sarah's bed, to make sure that the curious imp was falling back to sleep, then lit the bedside candle. The reflection of the small flame made her grey eyes glimmer. Turning the pouch over and over, she sank to the floor, using her bed to screen her movements.

An inbred sense of rectitude caused her to examine the pouch closely before opening it. No marks identifying the owner showed on the smooth leather. As she undid the cord that held the two flat sides of the pouch together, she wondered anew why someone would throw anything of value out of a carriage window. She flipped the pouch open. The drawing of a tulip was embossed in the leather. No name, just the tulip.

Some papers were stuffed into the side pockets of the pouch. With reluctance she drew the papers out. It was as if she were peeking into the private places of someone's life.

On the outside of the first folded sheet of paper a pair of flowers had been drawn. The same tulip etched on the leather packet was drawn on the upper left corner of the paper, as if one flower were the sender and the other the receiver. The arrangement of the flowers struck her as important, and she filed this clue away in the hodgepodge of information in her mind. Her father often told her that she would do well to organize her thoughts and strive for a more orderly existence.

She shoved her father's strictures aside. He would surely have something to say about the impropriety of examining someone's property without permission. Yet the need to know more took strong hold of her. She slid her thumbnail under the wax wafer affixed to the back of the sheet. The plain seal held for a moment, then broke, leaving behind a small piece of wax.

Julia sighed. There would be no hiding the fact that she'd pried the seal open. She smoothed out the sheet of paper on her lap. A list of names, followed by drawings of different flowers, ran down the page. Next to each flower was a letter of the alphabet and a number, like a code.

At the bottom of the sheet a message had been scrawled: "The newest blooms for the garden. I shall plant them soon."

She again read the names, then stared back at the cryptic words, trying to understand their meaning. Her gaze moved to the pouch. She looked through the rest of the papers. Some had very official-looking seals on them. These caused her a bit of alarm and she decided not to open them. But when she came upon a folded map she examined it. Points on the map were marked by flowers. It was all so curious.

She sat thinking for a time. When her candle began to sputter from the pooling of wax, she stirred. She tucked the papers back into the pouch. Quietly she left the room and went down the hall. In a few minutes she returned without the pouch.

She finished putting her things away and hid the portmanteau. As she dressed for bed in the soft pink nightgown which she had intended to wear for Harry, her thoughts turned again to him. He did not deserve to see the fine, sheer material float around her hips. She looked down and thanked Providence that the man had not come. She would never have let him see her, every rounded curve and shadowed part of her, in this diaphanous bit of cloth. It was indecent.

Had Harry possessed more than brotherly fondness for her she might have felt differently. For years they had been chums. When her brother, Lucian, came home on leave they went everywhere together—well, perhaps not *everywhere*. There was that time when the two fellows went up to Town for a ruinous weekend . . .

Julia wiped the beginnings of a tear from her eye. Maybe the reason for Harry's defection was that he had begun to remember why he had never taken such a step before. It only took some chance remark to bring it all back to him.

His pride, his blasted pride, she thought as she got into bed. Their arrangement might have worked. Surely it would have been better than being shackled to Oglesby.

She flung her arm over her face, trying to blot out the future. Perhaps her bruised, swollen eye would slow down the rush of events; she trusted that her mother's zealous regard for appearances would not fail.

To untangle all the bewildering happenings of the night, she would need time. But time was becoming quite precious to her. She felt as if her life would end in two weeks, instead of just begin, as her mother kept telling her.

"Harry," she whispered into the darkness, "where are you? Devil take you! I need you."

At that moment she cared little if her words were unfit for a lady to utter. Everything had gone wrong.

With a disgusted sigh, she realized that perhaps the outcome of the night had been for the best. She was not the one for Harry. Though it was a melancholy prospect, she knew she would have to do her duty.

She turned on her side and buried her cheek in her pillow. She stared at the small token ring on her finger, then grimaced at it. If there was a way out of this tangle, she swore she would find it.

It began to rain. "A fitting end to a putrid night," she muttered. The rain was merely a sign of the Creator's displeasure with ladies who tried to go against the will of their parents. It all came about from trying to elope.

TWO RIDERS DISMOUNTED a short distance from the old oak. Before lighting the lamp he carried, the taller and leaner of the two looked about to be sure they were alone. In the dark hours before dawn it became difficult to distinguish the form of a man from that of a tree.

The tall one eyed the surrounding area slowly, not moving from where he stood. He listened for any disturbance in the soft night sounds. Satisfied that they were indeed alone, he bent over his lamp and struck his flint close to the wick. Fixing the shutter to allow only a small stream of light to fall upon the ground, he moved the lamp in a slow, sweeping movement as he stepped nearer to the large oak tree. His companion followed him.

A few feet from the tree he stopped. With the swift motion of a man in prime condition, he knelt upon the ground and examined the markings left in the dirt.

"Looks like someone's been afore us," his companion commented as he peered over the man's shoulder.

The tall man stood and moved closer to the oak. He stopped again and again to examine the still-fresh tracks.

"Appears to be a woman's footprints," his companion offered.

"A long-limbed one at that," the man with the lamp replied. "Notice the distance between her paces. Not large-footed though." His fingertips touched the outer edge of one of the impressions in the dirt. "She's not heavy, very light on her feet."

They moved on. The one trailing behind pulled up short. "The lass fell." He pointed to the markings in the earth. A hand print from where she had helped herself up took his notice. "Nice long fingers."

"A lady perhaps?"

The stout companion nodded his head. "Could be."

At the oak tree there was evidence that something heavy had been on the ground near the trunk. A bag of some sort? Footprints led away from the clearing.

"Where's the scarf that the maid said she threw from the coach?" the stout one asked.

"The woman appears to be a likely candidate." The tall man straightened. "Her tracks are quite recent. You had better go back and give your assistance to Minns. I'll contact you soon."

"What mischief will you be up to?"

"Why, Scully, one would think you consider me a fribble, up to every lark in the county. While you take your little jaunt about the countryside, I shall be hard at work following our charming wood nymph." Bidding his companion Godspeed, he began to trace the prints from the clearing. He came out upon a foot lane, where her tracks turned right. He followed them to a gap in a yew hedge. A large house stood in the distance.

At that moment the heavens opened and the rain began to fall. The drops made marks like pox in the dust of the lane. Soon the footprints were beaten away. This was a curse and a blessing. He could not follow her, but then no one else could either.

The tall gentleman returned to his horse. Before mounting the stallion, he drew the lamp up to his face to blow out the flame. A patch of silver caught the light and winked into the darkness.

CHAPTER THREE

THE SUN SPARKLED on the panes of the long windows as it streamed into the breakfast parlour. Stretched out in the morning sunlight lay a large hound, his front paws tucked under his jaw.

Bounder, a mastiff weighing a good twelve stone, had joined the Witton family a few months past when Lucian, the second son, bestowed him as a gift. Already the dog was considered an honorary member of the family. His manners were quite correct, which secured his place in the household and gave him privileges not enjoyed by every canine.

His tail began to thump the floor when the door leading into the breakfast parlour swung inward. Cleeves, the butler, held open the door as the lady of the house passed into the room.

"Good morning, Cleeves," Amanda Witton called, as she crossed to the large, round table by the windows. Her cream-coloured muslin gown swayed around her willowy form as she took the chair that Cleeves held for her. "The bishop will be down presently. I shall wait for him."

"Very good, madam." He placed her morning mail before her and began a stiff retreat.

"Why Cleeves, whatever is the matter? You seem out of sorts this morning."

"Pardon, madam. I slept fitfully last night. I do miss being at the Palace."

"As do we all, but until the Palace is repaired no good can be served by repining."

Cleeves nodded gloomily. He did not wonder at the mistress's severity over the matter. She had been the one whose foot had gone through the floor. She vowed never to set foot, so to speak, in Bishop's Palace until the necessary improvements were made, which entailed a lengthy period of time, considering the age and disrepair of the structure.

The large manor house in which they currently resided would do until the family could return to the Palace, but it wasn't the same. Cleeves often hoped that the long-absent relation who leased the house to the family would return and demand his residence back.

"Cleeves, this melancholy will not do. 'Tis a glorious morning. The rain last night has made everything quite fresh and new smelling. I want you to do away with your sullens."

"Very good, *madam*." His lips pulled into an expression close to a smile.

At the sound of a familiar tread in the hall, Amanda raised her eyes from the invitation she was glancing at. Emory Witton, Lord Bishop of Bath and Wells, entered the room and crossed to his wife's side. His angular frame moved with courtly grace.

"A fine morning, my dear," he said, taking her hand in his. He lowered his head, glowing with silvery strands, and touched his lips to the back of her hand.

That was one of the many things that Amanda found endearing about her husband. He was gallant after nearly thirty years of marriage.

"Do not let me interrupt you, my dear," the bishop adjured. "By the looks of it you've a bit of correspondence there." He took his place beside his wife, set aside his stack of personal mail, then turned to the previous day's copy of the *Times*, which had arrived by the night mailcoach.

Amanda watched her husband with a fond eye. One of his most sterling qualities was his consistency. From the first morning after their marriage, breakfast had become a family ritual, just as reading the *Times* had. Amanda enjoyed consistency. She found great pleasure in knowing that at a certain hour one could expect this or that to occur. Such a regimented day ensured that one would never be caught doing something unusual. A bishop's wife had to be circumspect in her doings and those of her family.

Setting the invitation apart from the others, Amanda picked up a closely written letter from the Reverend Atley Oglesby. "Mr. Oglesby has written at last," she said, opening the missive. "He says that he has been detained from visiting us as his uncle required his attendance. He shall be joining us soon, though." She peered close to read the small writing on the page. "He sends his kindest regards to Julia and wishes to assure her his sentiments have not changed."

"A pity." The bishop frowned. "Say what you will, my dear, but your friend, Lady Clapton, served us ill when she put forward her godson as a fitting suitor for Julia."

Amanda bit her lip. "You must know that I would never have fallen in with her plan had I not known Mr. Oglesby when he was a child. Such engaging manners he had then, and a visage that would shame a cherub. How he can have changed so is a puzzle."

She was distracted by the merry sound of feminine chatter, which heralded the arrival of Faith, a gentle-eyed young lady in her twenty-first year, and Marion, who had just enjoyed her first season in Town. The girls dutifully kissed their parents before taking their seats.

"Where are your sisters, Faith?" Amanda asked.

The brown-haired beauty draped her napkin on her lap before answering. "Sarah is coming, but Julia has yet to rise." She received a sharp jab from Marion.

"Julia has not risen? Is she ill?" A worried look came into Amanda's eyes.

"Not ill, precisely," Marion interjected.

"Then what precisely is she?" the bishop asked, lowering his paper and giving his daughters his unnerving look.

The girls glanced at each other. "She's not quite herself this morning, Father," Marion said. "Is it my turn to offer the prayer?"

The bishop gave his daughters a long, silent stare before bowing his head. The ladies of his family exchanged a hasty look of understanding, then followed his example.

As the prayer ended, Sarah sidled into the room. Bounder stirred from his place on the rug and escorted her to her chair. She moved to her father and bestowed her token of regard. As her lips met his cheek, his arms slipped about her waist and he held her to his side.

"You are late, Sarah." He looked calmly into her eyes.

Sarah looked away, then down at the floor. "I ask your pardon, Father. I hope I have not inconvenienced you and Mama."

"I would have you read Bentley's sermon on the laxity of youth," the bishop ordered. The three young ladies grimaced.

"All of it, Father?" Sarah's voice dropped despondently.

"The first twenty pages will do. You may report to me tomorrow morning."

"Yes, Father." Sarah's bottom lip drooped when she brushed it against her mother's cheek. Breakfast began quietly.

The meal was nearly over when Cleeves ushered in Betty, the personal maid to the bishop's daughters. Betty dropped a quick curtsey and said, "Beg your pardon, my lord Bishop, but I felt it my duty to come to you at once. 'Tis Miss Witton. She's had an accident."

Amanda cried out and sprang to her feet. "The wedding! My poor Julia. Betty, what has happened?"

"I can't say, ma'am. Miss Witton won't tell me."

"Perhaps we should go up and see for ourselves," the bishop said.

"No!" Sarah jumped out of her chair, then recalled herself. "That is, I'm sure that Betty has mistaken the matter. Julia looked fine before I came down. All of this fuss over a silly accident."

The bishop looked at his youngest offspring. He rose from his chair and turned to Betty.

"Milord, I think you should see for yourself," Betty said, managing to send a frown in Sarah's direction. "In all my days of service to the young ladies, I have yet to see such an injury. 'Tis most unusual."

"Betty, you alarm me! My dear," Amanda said to her husband, "we must go at once to our daughter." She hurried from the room. The bishop and the maid followed.

"Sarah, you're all chatter and no thought." Marion glared at her sister. "If you'd kept your tongue still, we might have diverted the issue. Now, Father and Mama are full of suspicion. They won't rest until they have the truth."

"Poor, poor Julia," Faith said, shaking her head sadly. "However will she explain away her unsightly condition?"

"I, for one, shall be there to give what aid I can," proclaimed Sarah. She looked defiantly at her older sisters. "Are you with me?"

"We wouldn't let you go up there alone," Faith said, her voice trembling just a bit. She hated being brave.

Marion walked quickly to the door. "We're going with you to make sure you don't make matters worse." She elbowed Sarah behind her. "Just be quiet and Julia may come off unscathed."

"By the light of day, Marion," Sarah retorted, "keep those sharp elbows to yourself. You always do that, and I hate it."

"If we don't hurry we shall be too late." Faith pushed her sisters before her, using them as a buffer should any harsh parental words come her way.

At the door of the young ladies' bedchamber, Betty showed the bishop and his lady into the cheerful room, then she bobbed a curtsey and withdrew. Julia turned from her dressing table. She faced her parents squarely.

Amanda gasped and sank into the nearest chair. She stared at Julia's face, held speechless by what she saw.

"Daughter, what has happened to your eye?" The bishop moved closer to Julia. "It looks as if you've been bouting with a pugilist."

Amanda moaned and sought her handkerchief.

"I would rather not talk about it. 'Twas a ridiculous accident that should not have occurred." Julia looked at her father, willing him to understand and not ask questions.

The bishop remained quiet for a moment. He exhaled slowly, a preponderance of meaning in that long stream of air. "I see."

"You do?" Amanda and Julia asked together.

The bishop turned his back on them and began a thoughtful pacing. While he was thus engaged, Marion quietly led her sisters into the room. They tried to blend in with the furniture.

"Julia," Amanda began after several minutes of strained silence, "have you tried to cover it with rice powder?" She looked worriedly at her daughter. "Whatever has come over you of late? Here you are to be wed to a most upstanding man of the Church, and you conduct yourself like a hoyden. I had thought you'd given up your riotous ways long ago. But now...well, Mr. Oglesby will settle you. He shall be arriving in time for our Midsummer Eve festivities."

"Mother," Julia began in a halting voice. "I must speak to you about this wedding of mine. I truly believe that a three-month engagement period is...much too short a time to be considered seemly. What will people say?"

"Say? Why, my dear, all of our friends and relations were beside themselves with joy upon hearing the news of your betrothal." Amanda smiled overbrightly. "They had begun to think of you as an old mai— They thought that you might not find your heart's desire."

"Mr. Oglesby?" questioned Marion and Sarah in unison.

Amanda gave her daughters a hard stare. "The settlements have been signed and the invitations have been sent. Nothing can stop the wedding from taking place in— Is it only a fortnight away?"

"Yes," the Witton girls answered, as if one in voice and feeling. The three younger sisters looked with sympathy at the eldest.

"Mr. Oglesby might have corrected his problem with the spots by now," Sarah said, trying to offer a bit of solace.

"Should we increase your reading to thirty pages?" The bishop directed a pointed look at his youngest daughter.

"Excuse me, Father," Julia interjected, "but you have never, ah, taken measures of correction when we have spoken the truth. Mr. Oglesby does have a tendency to break out in spots."

"After you are married I am sure his pustular bent shall cease." Amanda leaned towards Julia and lowered her voice. "We shall talk of these delicate matters later—in private."

"Yes, Mama." Julia's brow wrinkled with thought. "I do believe we'll have to postpone the wedding, though. My bride's clothes will never be ready in time."

"I'll hire a few of the local women to help with the sewing," Amanda shot back.

"My eye might not be healed in a fortnight."

"Nonsense! The wedding will go as planned. What would people say if we drew back at this date?" Amanda went on to answer her own question. "I'll tell you what would be said. Word would spread that Mr. Oglesby didn't find you to his liking and was trying to end the connection. I grant that the match isn't all that we expected. But you have been so particular about men that something had to be done. You shall marry Mr. Oglesby, and that is that."

"Is there some reason that you cannot marry him, Julia?" The bishop's eyes were full upon her.

She looked down. How could she tell him that she doubted Oglesby's ability to inflame her passions? A gently reared lady did not speak of such things with her father, especially when he was a bishop. Sentiment might have been tolerated if she were a few years younger. But matters of the heart ceased to be important when the lady in question was still sitting on the shelf while younger sisters waited to be settled.

The refinement of Mr. Oglesby's mind, the political party he supported, his prospects, his devotion to the Church and his family connections would far outweigh his deficiencies of person and manner. That her mother had been, in a way, duped into accepting the match with good grace, and was now determined to conceal her feelings, was a lowering thought. It was Julia's duty to uphold her mother in the matter.

"Well, Julia?" The bishop's voice dropped to a kindly tone.

"I can give no reason, Father."

Amanda sat back in her chair with a sigh. "You see, my dear, she's merely experiencing a young bride's nervous spell. The excitement of the moment, I assure you."

"Oh, assuredly the excitement of the moment," remarked Sarah, the timbre of her voice edging toward sarcasm. The bishop's undeviating attention caused her to slide down in her chair.

"Sit up, Sarah," her mother admonished.

The bishop's attention moved from Sarah to Julia. "This matter concerning your eye is not settled. I will see you in my bookroom."

Shortly after morning prayers, the bishop and Julia met in the library. As he sat behind his massive desk, the bishop looked imposing and omniscient. The large window at his back, with the light streaming over his head and shoulders, played up this air of supremacy. With the bright sunlight shining in her face and shadowing his, Julia felt at a distinct disadvantage. Any attempt to hoodwink him would prove fruitless.

"Does your eye still cause you pain?"

His deep, soft voice chilled her. "A little pain now and then."

"Something must have hit it with quite a bit of force. The bruise is not too bad as I see it in the light here. I've seen worse." The bishop leaned back in his chair. "You may not know this, but when in Town I have upon occasion stepped around to watch the sparring at Gentleman Jackson's."

Her eyes widened with surprise—but not for long. She placed a hand on her bruised eye, finding the display of any sudden emotion to be a painful ordeal. Yet, that her father, a proper and staid gentleman, actually participated in the manly arts gave her quite a start.

She could sense his reaction to her look of surprise. She even envisioned one of his rare smiles, screened from her view now because of the direction of the sunlight.

"Will you tell me how you got the black eye?"

Her countenance waxed thoughtful. Her straight thin brows rose in hope, only to plunge in doubt. On her lap her long-fingered hands moved restlessly. "Father, I..." She shook her head. "I cannot tell you."

A long silence descended. Julia held herself firmly in check.

"I see," he said in his softest tone. Again there was silence.

Julia began to squirm in her straight-backed chair. Her hands became moist and her throat dry. The time seemed to crawl by.

A tap on the door brought blessed relief. Cleeves entered and quietly moved to his master's side. He presented a sealed letter. "A messenger brought this, milord, and he awaits a reply."

The bishop took the missive and examined the seal. His thick, silvery brows elevated. He broke the seal and spread the letter out before him on the desk.

"Cleeves, ask my lady wife if I might have a few moments of her time. Tell her I await her pleasure." As Cleeves left to fetch Mrs. Witton, the bishop turned to Julia. "You have a reprieve, miss. I will say this, your mother would be most distressed if scandal were to become attached to our name. I'll not question you further about your activities of last night. Your history of misadventures is quite well known to me. Just see that you refrain from upsetting your mother."

"I shall do my best to obey your wishes," Julia said, her voice carrying a hint of doubt. She paused thoughtfully. "Father—"

Before Julia could continue, the door flew open and Amanda rushed to her husband's side, saying, "My dearest, what is it? Fateful tidings? I was with Cook when Cleeves brought your message." The bishop stood and caught hold of her fluttering hands. "You needn't give me the news gently. It must be of great import, else why would you summon me here to your bookroom, which you have never done before?" Amanda squeezed his hands. "Have pity, Emory. Tell me! Is it Lucian?"

Julia went to her mother's side and helped ease her to a chair. She picked up her father's discarded *Times* from the desk and began to wave it vigorously before her mother's face. "Now, Mama, do not overset yourself." She looked up at her father.

"My dear wife, a calamity has not befallen us. Lucian is hale and hearty, God willing." He took Amanda's listless hand. "I have disrupted your morning routine. I ask your forgiveness, my dear."

"If nothing has occurred, then why did you summon me?" Amanda clutched her hand over her heart.

The bishop cleared his throat. "I've only moments ago received a message from Lord Rossiter."

"Has someone in *his* family died?" Amanda's brow wrinkled. "Does he want you to officiate at the funeral?"

"Amanda, my sweet, these flights of fancy are soaring beyond what is reasonable. Lord Rossiter has asked if he may presume on his acquaintance with me by seeking permission to inspect the cathedral library for some bits of obscure information."

"You called me in here for *that*?"

"He begs our indulgence for the short notice," the bishop went on as if his wife had not spoken. "It seems that his research has led him to Wells. He shall be arriving this very day."

"Today!" Amanda put her hand to her head, then drew a deep breath. "I daresay it can be done. Flowers. I've heard that he has some unusual interest in flowers. He is quite odd, I am told." The instincts of a mother with daughters for whom to provide husbands surged through her, giving her renewed energy. "Still, he is an eligible gentleman, and a peer. We shall have him bide here with us while he dabbles in these studies of his. The girls will find it pleasing, I am sure, to share his company."

"Invite him here? My dear, you forget that in a mere fortnight we will be up to our ears in a wedding."

"What does that signify? The presence of Lord Rossiter, a hero and a bachelor, will only enhance the celebration. My dear bishop, surely you can see the advantage of having his lordship here with us? You must send a message to him at once."

An amused glint lit the bishop's eyes. "What do you suggest I say, my love?"

"What should you say? My dear, insist he come. Say we feel duty bound to have him as our guest. Extend our hospitality and say whatever is necessary to get the man here." She saw the satisfied smile which played around her husband's mouth. "Emory, you scoundrel! Manoeuvring your own wife into getting just what you desired. For shame, I say!" Her stern expression began to twitch. Before she lost her dignity, she made her exit from the room.

Julia looked from the closing door to her father. A gentle smile curved his lips. He turned again to the letter before him and read. Quietly she began to move to the door.

"Julia."

She stopped. Turning, she met her father's eyes. "Sir?"

"I would say this before I dismiss you. Your mother's happiness means a great deal to me. Consider carefully what you are about before you place yourself and your family in a position of embarrassment. If you discover that you have had a change of heart be sure that change has occurred for the right reasons, not merely a quaking of nerves."

"I shall do my duty, Father."

He placed his fingertips together and peered at her over them. "Mr. Oglesby's family is one of consequence. Though his godmother has conducted herself less than honourably in this affair, your betrothed must be held blameless. He is a gentleman. He is aware of his duties to the Church and to his parishioners. He is well connected. Do not let a momentary weakness blind you to these fine qualities."

"Father—" She gathered her courage. "—I do not love him."

A heavy silence descended between them. At last the bishop looked up from his hands, and said, "I see. My child, I shall not force you into wedlock. But consider this: at times, that sentiment grows *after* the vows are spoken. Wait until you have spent more time in Mr. Oglesby's company before setting your mind upon an irretrievable course. His purpose in coming before the wedding is to better his acquaintance of you. A deeper affection will grow from a more thorough knowledge of each other." He waved her out, and returned to Rossiter's missive.

Later that morning, Amanda met Julia on the stairs. "Oh, my dear, I know I am forgetting something." Amanda totted her list on her fingers. "I have sent Faith and Marion to tend to the flowers, Sarah is in the breakfast parlour reading her sermon, the maids are airing the large drawing room, and Cook is sending for more food. If you would direct the maids in the Red Rooms, then I could consult with Cook about the revised menu.''

"The Red Rooms! You cannot mean to use them."

"Why ever not?" Amanda asked, affronted.

"Mama, those rooms are seldom used. You've said, times out of memory, that they are the State Rooms, set aside for notables such as the Archbishop or the Prince Regent. Not a rakish peer who dabbles in horticultural studies.''

"Lord Rossiter *is* a notable. A war hero. A Knight of the Garter." She caught hold of Julia's square chin. "Apply some more rice powder around your eye."

"I did. It cannot cover the thing, yet."

"'Tis a mercy that it is not worse." Amanda looked closely at the blackened eye. "Perhaps in a few days you will look more presentable for receiving company, but until then I must ask you to keep to your room while his lordship is with us. What an odd appearance you present with that eye. And we can give no logical reason for its condition?''

"No, Mama, we cannot."

Amanda gave her a frustrated look, then sent her off to the Red Rooms.

On the threshold of the suite of rooms, containing an antechamber, a dressing-room, and a bedchamber, Julia surveyed a pair of maids and a footman busily at work. The rooms were overflowing with flowers of every sort.

Julia ordered things to her liking. She moved around, running her hand over the wood surfaces, making the servants a little nervous. Her inspection led her into the dressing-room. She moved nonchalantly to the clothes-press and reached up to the top. Her fingers brushed only the upper woodwork of the piece of furniture.

"Julia! Julia!" Sarah called from the antechamber. She raced into the room. "He's here! You must see his lordship's chaise. It's a bang-up turnout."

"He is here so soon?" Julia's shoulders drooped.

"Yes, he must have been waiting at the Crown or the Angel for Father to send him word. Come on!" Sarah grabbed Julia's hand and pulled her from the room, out into the corridor and along to the hall. At the stairs, the two young ladies stopped in midflight.

In the hall below, Cleeves was taking a tall-crowned beaver hat from their honoured guest. He handed it to a footman and bade his lordship to follow him.

Lord Rossiter stood with his back to Julia and Sarah. The excellent cut of his coat showed off the breadth of his shoulders and the trimness of his waist. To Julia, a lady above middling height, his impressive size seemed to complement his appearance; and she thought it pleasing that he was not a big bear of a man, but long and lean.

He glanced up the staircase and paused, his attention seemingly caught by the portrait of a Witton ancestor. Julia and Sarah drew back from the rail as Lord Rossiter turned to follow the butler. A shaft of light caught the silver patch, which his lordship wore over his left eye. The patch seemed to wink up at the bishop's daughters.

"Did you ever see such a man?" Sarah asked in awed tones. Her question went unanswered. Julia turned away and hurried back to the Red Rooms.

CHAPTER FOUR

"LORD ROSSITER," Cleeves announced from the doorway of the large drawing room. He stepped aside to allow the lean, fine-muscled lord to make his entrance.

Thomas John Brainard, Baron Rossiter of Rossiter—the honours and titles recently bestowed upon him by the Crown—paused on the threshold. It was said that he took great pride in his dress. The cut of his coat, the precise knot of his cravat and the shine of his Hessian boots proclaimed him a fellow of Brummell's school. In his graceful hand he held a silver-headed cane. With his other hand he raised a quizzing-glass to his uncovered blue eye. The silver patch he wore on the other seemed to mock the world, and it was accompanied by a thin scar, which trailed over his cheek-bone to stop an inch or so from the edge of his mouth.

His effect upon Amanda was profound. "Oh, my... Dear me!" For a moment she seemed only to see the patch and scar, and gathering her wits, she began to fan herself briskly. A peer was a peer, she reasoned, as she smiled encouragingly at Faith and Marion, who were seated next to her on the sofa in an attractive family grouping.

The bishop stepped forward to greet their guest. "Lord Rossiter, welcome," he said, as he extended his hand.

"So kind of you to humour one of my whims, my lord bishop." Rossiter took the bishop's hand. For a long moment they gazed at each other in a measuring way.

The introductions were soon completed, but not before Faith had blushed a vivid pink when she encountered the bright blue eye, magnified by the quizzing-glass. Her smile froze on her face.

"I must beg your forgiveness, Mrs. Witton," Rossiter began after taking a seat, "for coming upon you in this unseemly fashion. But when I am on the scent of a species I find my manners those of a country bumpkin. It was most kind of you to offer the hospitality of your home during the term of my research. Fascinating subject, flowers." He smiled coolly at Faith and Marion. "But I see you have some lovely blooms of your own."

The bishop shot Rossiter a dubious glance. This was not the man he had met three years before. Of course, that had been prior to the wound, the patch and the title. But no man could change so from a hardened soldier to a modish fop without a reason for the metamorphosis.

After receiving a blank look in return from the baron, the bishop settled back next to Amanda, content to await what would develop.

"How kind of you, my lord," Amanda said, quite oblivious to the exchange between the two men. "I've two more blooms..." She turned pink with embarrassment. "Ah, that is, I've two more daughters whom you will meet later." She smiled in a satisfied manner and offered refreshments to her guest.

When Cleeves arrived with the tea tray, Faith was given the honour of seeing to his lordship's needs. She handed him his dish of brew in a pretty manner. For her efforts she received a thorough going over by the bright blue orb, which she later told her sisters was a most chilling experience.

"We did not see you in Town during the Season, Lord Rossiter." Amanda was genuinely puzzled. "Mayhap there was reason?"

"My studies so rarely bring me into polite society, Madam. This last spring I was tracing the source of a particular species of lily. Fascinating!"

"I daresay," murmured Amanda. "Such a shame. Nevertheless, we often saw Mrs. Fitzsimmons, who I believe is your sister."

A darkening look fell over his lordship's face. "My *step*sister has always enjoyed Town life."

"I hope the Season was not too tiring for her. One could count on meeting the dear lady at every affair of importance, looking so lovely with her escort, that very handsome French *émigré*."

"When last I saw her, Trixie was looking a bit pulled. She's taking a repairing lease in the country."

Amanda noticed the whitening around the knuckles that held the silver-headed cane. "Have you had a long journey, my lord?"

"From Bath merely. If I appear a bit fatigued...my studies kept me from my bed last night. Simply fascinating! I could scarcely tear myself away."

"My dear," the bishop broke in before Amanda could express her sentiments upon such studious habits, "would you excuse Lord Rossiter and myself? I wish a few moments of private speech with him before I go about my duties today. The hour is already advanced."

"My dear bishop, say no more," Amanda stood. Her daughters followed suit and took their leave. Once out of the drawing-room, Amanda sent the girls about their daily pursuits and she went to consult her calendar.

no concern of mine. After all, only some people believe that a promise is a promise."

"Sarah, what is all this jobation about?" Marion asked.

Harry looked at the girl. "What *has* happened to Julia?" The two young ladies at his side shifted uncomfortably. "What's this? She wasn't caught—"

"No!" Sarah cried, before Harry could say any more. "She *hasn't* caught anything infectious. She has been laid up with a slight malady. A trifling indisposition. Should be fit as a horse any day." She held out the reins to Harry. "We must dress for dinner. We have a guest, you know. Do call again when you next visit your father."

"Yes, Harry, see if you cannot get a long furlough." Faith tugged at his arm encouragingly. "The War Office works you far too hard."

"I like to feel useful," he replied, his gaze moving to his half-empty sleeve.

"Oh, Harry, don't!" Marion turned to face him. "You are the finest man I know. Why, anyone would be proud to be—"

He stepped away from her as he gave a disparaging laugh that kept Marion from finishing. Harry swept the girls a gallant bow and mounted his horse. "My dears, if I ever found a woman who could love me the way I am, then, by heaven, I'd pluck her up and toss her in the saddle before me."

"*We* love you, Harry," Faith affirmed.

"Like a demned brother, my angel, but that's not what I am looking for in a wife." And with that he spurred his horse and galloped down the gravel drive.

THAT EVENING, while the family was occupied in the drawing room with their guest, Harry returned to the manor house. This time he entered through the gardens.

The sun sat low on the horizon, and dark shadows had begun to stretch over the small park that surrounded the manor. Harry had enough cover to creep about the grounds without being seen from the windows that faced the gardens. He found Julia sitting on the stone railing of the summerhouse. They looked at each other.

"You blackguard!" She shot a wrathful glance at him before turning away. But during that glance her face had come out of the shadows.

Harry lunged forward and grabbed her chin. "What in blazes happened to your eye?"

"A little late for concerning yourself about me, my buck. By heaven, where were you last night? I waited and waited. And what was my reward for such diligence? A black eye! If you could not stand the thought of marrying me, dunderhead, then you need only have said so when we planned this hare-brained scheme." She curled her hand into a fist and waved it under his nose. "I ought to darken *your* daylights. Now, in a fortnight I shall become Mrs. Atley Oglesby."

"Did you attempt reasoning with your father?"

She levelled a cutting look in Harry's direction, then held up the hand with Oglesby's ring on it. "As you see, it was quite useless. Father wants me to know the man better, and then learn to love him." She turned away as she felt a lump gather in her throat.

"Julia, I could not saddle you for life with a cripple."

"A cripple!" She turned and caught his hand. "That's . . . that's balderdash! You are not a cripple."

He kissed her forehead, then looked down at her eye. "No round tales, my dear girl. I want the truth. How did you get the shiner?"

"I got it from a passing stranger."

"Someone accosted you!" Harry's soft brown eyes took on a murderous look.

"No, but that could have happened, too. Last night was a farcical escapade. I should have known better than to attempt anything so featherheaded." A disgusted sigh slipped from deep within her chest. She commenced to relay the events of her early-morning vigil. "But the most singular thing of all was the pouch that hit me." She touched her eye.

"A pouch hit you?"

"A pouch wrapped in a scarf."

"A pouch wrapped in a scarf," he muttered, looking at her as if she had just escaped from Bedlam.

"You don't believe me! This is not something one makes up. It happened!" She went on to explain about the pouch and its contents, then said, "Harry, some of the seals looked like those used by the Crown. I've seen them before when Father has received missives from London. And don't forget the list of names and the map."

"Where is this packet?"

She turned away from him. "It is hidden. I cannot get to it at the moment." She paced for a time, then rounded on him. "What am I to do? I cannot tell Father I was out attempting to elope last night when I was hit by a pouch that might contain secret documents. He would have me married to Oglesby by the cock's next crow. A flighty daughter is not highly thought of in a bishop's establishment."

"Nothing so settling as marriage, hey?"

"Do not talk to me of marriage, you jilt! If the notion of tying the knot with me is so repugnant to you, then I daresay I shall have to take Oglesby." She walked away from him, giving him a martyred glance over her shoulder.

"If you'd like, we can leave now and make for the Border."

She looked at him and smiled, shaking her head. "I have had time to think. It has come to me that we know each other far too well to be married happily. Besides, Father said he would be most displeased if something occurred to overset Mama. I would bring down his severe displeasure upon us both if I bolted with you now." She looked toward the house and sighed. "He knows I was up to something last night, but he has not discovered what. I would rather he never knew. Father has a way of looking at one that crumbles the stiffest resolve."

Harry shuddered. "He does have that way about him. I remember how he looked when Lucian and I were sent down from school."

"Then try to imagine facing him after returning from Gretna Green." She smiled at Harry's low whistle. "A bishop's daughter simply does not elope. But I had to try, Harry. You understand, I had to try." She shivered. "I shall never forget my first meeting with Oglesby. The settlements had already been signed—by proxy of course. Lady Clapton had kept him hidden at his uncle's in Durham. She rhapsodized about his virtues until she had us all believing that I was most fortunate to have him. Then one day he walked into Lady Clapton's drawing room and..." She sighed.

"There, there, buck up, old girl. What would you have me do for you?"

"A small favour, truly."

Harry cocked a doubting brow at her. "As I recall those were the words you used when *you* suggested we run for the Border. What small favour is it this time?"

"I want you to go to London and look about. Discover what you can about messages embossed with flowers."

"Lud, girl! Have pity. I can't ask a fellow about flowers. I'd be taken up and put under treatment like the King."

"Then find out if there is any talk of missing plans or orders. Surely as a major attached to the War Office you would hear things, secret things."

"I make a point of not listening to titbits whispered about. But what if these papers you have belong to the French? I think you had better hand them over to me."

"I suppose I should, but then I so rarely do as I ought. As for the papers belonging to the French, I doubt it. The map looked to be of France and the writing was in English. We just need to be sure that when we hand over the pouch it is to the proper person. Until that time, I shall keep it."

"Julia..." Harry's voice held a threatening edge.

"Truly, the papers will be safer here. No one knows I have them."

"If those papers are important, someone will try to find them. I'd as lief it were me, not you, whom they came looking for in that event."

She considered the matter for a moment. "That may be, but, you see, the papers are in a place to which neither you nor I can gain access without giving away the whole sorry tale."

"Dash it, where the devil have you hid the thing?"

"In a place that is beyond my reach at the moment. That is all I will tell you."

"Stubborn woman! It goes against the grain and my better judgment, but I shall see what I can discover in Town." He began to stride away from her, but turned to deliver a parting shot. "One day you'll meet a man who won't stand for any of your sauce. I live to see the day."

"Tell me, what kept you from my side last night?"

He flashed her a wicked grin. "I stopped to celebrate my nuptials."

"And got foxed?"

"Thoroughly," he retorted, then walked off into the gathering darkness.

Julia's amusement faded to sadness as she crept back toward the house by the faint light of the rising moon. What was she to do about Oglesby? she wondered. Passing close to the terrace, she heard the tinkling notes of Faith at the pianoforte. The sweet, faintly sad music played upon Julia's mood. Drawing back out of sight of the windows, she found a nearby bench and sat down to listen to her sister's performance.

A footstep crunched in the gravel path, alerting her that she was not alone. She drew close to the box hedge that framed the back and sides of the bench. The end of a cane struck the ground before her and she gasped.

"Pardon, I thought I was alone out here. You gave me quite a start, miss." A bit of silver glimmered down at her.

"Lord Rossiter?" Julia peered up, then leaned closer to the hedge. She knew her mother would be most displeased if she let his lordship see her eye. After all, she was supposed to be in bed with some mysterious ailment.

"At your service." He bowed. "May I?" he asked, indicating the bench with his cane.

She moved to the very edge of the marble seat. Turning her face so that he could not see her eye, she shrank away from Lord Rossiter.

"I'll admit my phyz isn't a pretty sight, but I do think that sort of cringing indicates a lack of breeding."

"Oh, it isn't your phyz, it's mine. You see, I've had the... measles. I developed a terrible rash."

He leaned closer and tried to see her face. "Ma'am. I must suppose you are one of the bishop's daughters. The eldest, perhaps? The one with the infirmity?"

The words "eldest" and "infirmity" bothered her. "Yes, I am Miss Witton." She drew back further and placed her handkerchief up to her face. "I must withdraw, my lord. I am still considered infectious."

"Are you? That's of no consequence. I had 'em as a child. Should you be out of bed, though, and in this cool night air?"

She sighed, tired of the confines of her room. "There is nothing to do in bed."

"That is a matter of opinion," he murmured.

Julia chuckled softly. "I daresay a man of your vast experience has enough knowledge of such matters to have an opinion."

He looked at her closely and raised his quizzing-glass to his eye. "What a curious remark for a bishop's daughter to make."

"Why does being the daughter of a bishop make the remark curious?"

"One has come to expect—"

"Oh, yes," she returned, "Society has come to expect saintliness from the children of the clergy. I should tell you, my lord, that even the offspring of men of God have sentiments and thoughts of their own not found in a prayer book. I'll have you know that I haven't spent my entire life singing psalms."

Lord Rossiter looked at her in an amused way. "Take a damper, child."

"Child! I am four-and-twenty, sir."

"Are you now? You don't look it in the moonlight." He tipped her chin up a little, exposing the charming profile of her averted face. Even at four-and-twenty she had a look of freshness about her that was inviting.

"Remarkably preserved for one of such advanced years," he commented. "And honest, too."

She pulled out of his grasp. "Not always honest."

"This *is* remarkable, Miss Witton. You are even honest about being dishonest."

"This is nonsensical! I am not to be seen by you. I can imagine what Mama will say when she finds out."

"Then let's not tell Mama."

"Are you the devil's advocate, Lord Rossiter?" she asked, giving him a teasing smile. "You have a sardonic disposition. One might even say your aspect is diabolic." With his curly, short-cut dusky hair, seeming like horns, and the fierce-looking scar, he did indeed appear devilish.

The silver patch caught the moonlight and flashed out. The corner of his mouth curled upward. "You have a quick and deadly thrust, Miss Witton. I daresay the devil and I have had a close association at various times during my life. Does the daughter of a bishop find that disturbing?"

"No. The sinner isn't as unique as he thinks he is."

"Pinked by the lady!" He made a fencer's movement of concession. "Your mother has made a grave mistake in keeping such a prize hidden away. I am amazed that some intelligent fellow hasn't snapped you up."

"I have been snapped up," she replied dully. A pause fell upon their banter.

"Betrothed?"

"Yes."

"Who is the fortunate fellow?"

"Atley Oglesby."

"Who?"

"He is the rector of a parish in Durham."

"Sorry fellows, those devil-catchers. Yowling bores."

Turning her head, she hid her smile. In her heart she agreed with him. She forcibly restrained herself from giving voice to her sentiments. Mr. Oglesby was a problem that she would handle by herself.

Rossiter looked at the quiet young woman at his side. "Have I greatly offended you, Miss Witton?"

"Not at all. My sisters tell me that I am thick-skinned."

He ran his fingers up her arm until his progress was blocked by her short puffed sleeve. "I would not call it thick. Quite soft, actually. Yet, you've not too much flesh. One would not call you plump."

"Are you implying that I am raw-boned? A Long Meg?" she asked, tapping his hand away. The corners of her wide, full mouth quirked into an engaging smile. The smile began to fade as the music from the drawing-room died away into stillness. One of the long windows opened.

"My dear bishop," Amanda could be heard saying, "I merely wish to let in the cool night air. I am not spying on the man. But how long does it take to, as you say, commune with nature?" She turned from the casement and walked back into the room.

Julia stood and held out her hand, keeping her face turned from the light. "Good night, sir," she whispered. "I shall see you again when I am fully recovered." As he began to raise her fingers to his lips, she pulled away. "I must go." She moved quietly around the hedge and disappeared from sight at the corner of the house.

He watched her go, then jabbed at the ground with the tip of his cane. With hardly a thought of what he was about, he began to draw the shape of a flower in the dirt. It was a rose just beginning to open. He stared at his etching for a moment. When he stood to go and rejoin the others in the drawing-room, he obliterated the rose with the heel of his shoe. Then he walked away from the marble bench, dismissing the impossible.

"Lord Rossiter," Amanda exclaimed as he entered the room through a long window, "we were beginning to wonder if you had got lost in the darkness."

"No, madam, I was not lost in the darkness, but lost in the beauty of the garden bathed in moonlight. The scent of flowers drew me into the depths of nature's charm. You are to be complimented on your lovely roses. One bud particularly caught my fancy." Rossiter sat at his ease next to Faith and smiled coolly at her, the corners of his mouth lifting merely a jot.

CHAPTER FIVE

AMANDA FANNED HERSELF. She hardly knew how to take the man, what with all his talk of flowers and nature's charms. Since his return from viewing the garden the room seemed much cooler—a condition undoubtedly brought about by Rossiter's chill and distant nature. But if flowers interested him so, then she would talk of them. "Faith has a knack with flowers. She arranged all the bouquets in your rooms." She smiled proudly upon her daughter.

"Did she? How fascinating," he said, drawling the last word. Then he raised the quizzing-glass to his eye and looked Faith over with an interested air.

His action pleased Amanda. She was gratified by the attentions he paid her daughters. Apart from one or two peculiar traits, she found little wanting in him. He would do quite well for her Faith. The title was new, like so many since the outbreak of the war, but the family had made notable contributions to society since time out of mind. She knew many mamas with a coming manner, who had their eyes on Lord Rossiter. If he should find Faith to his liking, then Amanda would see that the knot was tied.

For the rest of the evening Amanda supervised their guest's entertainment. She went about this in the most unexceptional manner; Faith played sliver loo with Rossiter for chicken stakes while Marion read aloud. No one could have censured Amanda for being a bumptious mother, out to secure a husband for one of her girls. As a lady, she knew how to comport herself. The last thing she wanted said of her, a bishop's wife, was that she was scheming to nab a peer for a son-in-law. Heaven forbid!

And so it was that as the clock struck ten o'clock, Mrs. Witton rose to bid Lord Rossiter a good night. She gathered her daughters and left the gentlemen to amuse themselves. At the first landing, Faith and Marion wished their mother pleasant dreams. She climbed the stairs of the west wing and they went up to the east.

In the young ladies' bedchamber, Julia and Sarah sat up waiting. They were dressed in their night rails with their hair tumbling down about their shoulders. The bishop's daughters had hair of various shades of brown, Faith's being the darkest and Sarah's lightened by the sun.

"Well, when are the banns to be read?" Sarah asked pertly, as her two elder sisters entered the room. She plopped down on her bed and watched Faith and Marion undress.

"What a pack of nonsense you've been speaking today, Sarah," Faith retorted, as she took the pins from her hair.

"If you try to tell me Mama did not foist you upon his lordship, then you will be the one speaking nonsense." Sarah propped her hands under her chin. "I think he looks like an untrustworthy ne'er-do-well. I have never seen such a heartless looking man!"

"Now, you are being absurd," Julia said, helping Marion out of her gown. "He is quite uncommon."

"Heigh-ho!" Sarah bounced up to kneel upon her bed. "Has our Julia taken leave of her senses?"

"Julia," Faith began in a kindly tone, "even you must admit that the man is far from personable."

The eldest Witton girl eyed her sisters scornfully. "Look beyond the patch and scar, my dears, and you shall find a very interesting man."

"Ha! Flowers interesting? Ha!" Sarah squinted in doubt.

"It is all very well for you to say look beyond those things." Faith shuddered. "He was not staring at you all evening with his good eye. Lord Rossiter has a way of gazing out of that lazy blue orb that quite terrifies me."

"Well, that settles it," Sarah said. "Marion, it appears as if you shall be the one to go to his lordship."

"Sarah, give over, do." Marion turned and headed for her bed. After she had crawled under the bedclothes, she said, "*If* I wanted a brigand with a fop's taste in dress for my mate, then Lord Rossiter would do very nicely." She smiled at her sisters and pulled the covers over her head.

"I think the man's up to something smoky," Sarah stated ominously. "Any man who'd spend thirty minutes at dinner rambling on about wildflowers is touched in his upper works, or up to no good. If he's not here to marry one of you, then I say he is here to steal the silver, and I plan to alert Cleeves."

"Oh, no!" cried Faith, her voice fading away. "Not again, Sarah. Please, not again. The last time we had a guest you thought the poor man was after Mama's diamonds. I was never so mortified in my life."

"He looked smoky to me," averred Sarah.

"The man was entering the orders!" Faith's anguished voice rose an octave.

Sarah sniffed disdainfully. "That was merely a guise to hide his true purpose—Mama's diamonds!"

Emerging from under her blankets, Marion asked, "Just how many pages did you have to read after that unholy episode?"

Sarah tossed her head and maintained a stony silence.

"I think you had better restrict your spying to the servants," Julia said, smiling at her youngest sister.

"The servants! Oh, no—" Faith put a hand on her brow as she took to her bed. "Sarah, how could you!"

"Don't be so pious, Faith," Sarah advised. "I recall some of your escapades."

"Those were all Julia's fault." Faith looked to her elder for confirmation. "Weren't they?"

"'Tis most unfortunate that sisters have such long memories," Julia remarked in a good-natured fashion. "There is no telling what dark secret might slip out when one's siblings fall to reminiscing." She shook her head. "Most unfortunate."

"Unfortunate, indeed!" Sarah curled up between her sheets. "As if any of us would give the other away. I, for one, shall be loyal to all of you till my last breath."

"A worthy sentiment," Marion cast over her shoulder as she turned to face the wall, "from one who is known for letting her chatter land her own self—and others—in the suds."

"Enough," Julia said tersely, when Sarah rose up to retort. "If you are to look your best tomorrow for our esteemed guest, as I am sure Mama would wish, then sleep is needed." She went around blowing out the bedside candles. When darkness filled the room Julia went to one of the windows overlooking the garden. She drew back the curtain and gazed out upon the grounds.

Down at the far side of the garden, Lord Rossiter paced.

"You see," Sarah said, peering over Julia's shoulder, "he's up to some sort of devilry."

"Shhh. Go back to bed."

"Very well, but you keep watch over him. Wake me if he does anything peculiar."

Julia sat on the window seat and continued to watch Rossiter. She, too, wondered what he was about.

In the gentle night air Rossiter continued to pace. He pulled out his timepiece, holding it to allow the moonlight to fall upon its face. He pushed the piece back into his waistcoat pocket and resumed his pacing, punctuating the beat of his steps with his cane.

After a time the shadow of a man emerged from the trees bordering the garden. Rossiter turned at the man's furtive approach.

"I've bad news, milord," muttered Scully. "The little lady got away. Fair bamboozled me, she did."

"The devil!" Rossiter strode away, then back again. "How did it happen?"

"I was takin' her back to your place outside of Bath, followin' orders like you said. She gave me the slip at the Rusty Duck while I was tendin' to nature's business. Sorry, sir."

"She'll head straight for Philippe Vodrey. We'd best be ready for company, Scully."

"Aye. I'll keep me peepers open." Scully looked down at the ground and stuffed his hands into his pockets. "Appears Miss Trixie—ah, that is Mrs. Fitzsimmons—has gone the limit this time. But then she really ain't blood family. That aunt of hers must have twisted Miss Trixie's reason when she was growing up. A body wonders at these strange starts of hers."

Lord Rossiter put his hand on Scully's shoulder. "Be a good fellow and keep your wonderings to yourself. I'll be damned lucky to come out of this affair with the family honour intact."

"Well, she ain't a Brainard after all. Stepsister and all that—makes a difference."

"She is still my sister regardless."

Scully cleared his throat. "Ah, any luck yet findin' the pouch?"

"None. My man has questioned the staff in that quiet way that valets have and found nothing untoward there. He'll be searching their rooms tomorrow." Rossiter paused and rubbed his chin. "I think it is one of the daughters. I have ruled out the youngest; she isn't tall enough to be the one we tracked."

"Got a notion which one?"

"A notion, but no more than that."

"What about his lordship, the bishop? Will he be giving us any worry?"

"No."

"That's good. I've no fancy to mess with a man of the cloth. A body's got to draw the line somewhere, even in our profession."

"Scully, were you about the grounds earlier this evening when a young lady was out here?"

"Are you meaning the one who met the officer?"

"She met an officer?" Rossiter sounded surprised. "Are we talking about the same lady? The one I'm speaking of comes up to about here." He brushed the side of his head, just below his ear, with the tips of his fingers. "She's slender and her hair is light brown. She's been ill."

"The lady I saw looked the same. The officer called her Julia. I couldn't get close enough to make out anything else."

"These sisters all look very much alike. Yet, I don't recall a Julia in the bunch. The lady I'm speaking of is the eldest daughter." Rossiter paused and shook his head. "She cannot be the same woman that you saw. She's a lady. Ladies don't meet officers on the sly."

"They met in that stone summer-house at the back of the grounds. They were right friendly with each other. He kissed her."

Rossiter looked at Scully in an odd fashion. It could not be the same lady, he reasoned. Scully's information conflicted with what he had gleaned from the eldest Witton daughter. The girl was engaged to a rector. She had just recovered from the measles, or some such thing. Granted the young lady was out of the ordinary, but a clandestine meeting was another matter altogether. Kissing an officer in the summer-house, not likely!

"Just how many women in this house are stepping out with amorous bucks?" Rossiter asked in amusement.

"There's this comely maid who's seeing the groom. Now, those two were worth watchin'!"

"Scully, I think you enjoy your work too much. There are certain things in this life that ought to be given the privacy they deserve."

"If I'd turned a blind eye on you and that ladybird, 'twould a dead man you'd be today. That stiletto would have gone in your back 'stead of the cushion."

Rossiter's chuckle greeted this recollection. "You've got my undying gratitude, old fellow. But you must admit the lady was a rare handful."

"She was that." Scully grinned. "Who's the lovely you're dallying with this time, sir?"

The silver patch gleamed in the moonlight. "You're an impudent dog."

"Watch dogs get a bit brassy in their old age. But this ol' dog's given you the warning more than once when stray husbands and knives have come your way."

Rossiter clapped Scully on the shoulder and shook the rascally fellow warm-heartedly. "Your bones must be troubling you, old friend. You have not chewed on that one for an age. With any luck we shall have you back in front of your snug fire before the week's out. After all, how much trouble can the daughters of a bishop be?" He looked back at the manor house. "It appears the Witton household has settled for the night. My man will be along soon to relieve you of your duty. Tell him to look for un-invited guests." With an offhanded salute, Rossiter sauntered back toward the house, occupied with his thoughts. He did not see the curtain move back in place in the upper window of the young ladies' bedchamber.

CHAPTER SIX

ALL THROUGH BREAKFAST the next morning Lord Rossiter withstood the piercing stare directed at him by Sarah. The girl appeared fascinated by his patch. She did not take her eyes off him once during the meal. When he complimented Mrs. Witton on the lovely table she set, the girl's mouth dropped open and she stared.

"My grandmother gave Mama the silver as a bride's gift," Sarah stated. "It has been in the family for years and years. No one has dared to steal it."

Faith's and Marion's eyes widened. They looked at Sarah and tried to kick her into silence. A grimace of pain crossed Marion's face as her foot met with a chair leg. Faith scored a hit. Unfortunately it was Bounder that she kicked. The dog, curled up at Sarah's feet, let out a deep-throated yelp.

Amanda retained her composure in the midst of all the racket and offered the bishop another cup of tea. "Sarah, I daresay our silver holds no interest for Lord Rossiter," she remarked, trying to divert his lordship's attention from what was transpiring under the table.

"I wouldn't be too sure of that, Mama," Sarah gave Rossiter a suspicious glance.

Feigning an air of interest, Rossiter picked up a spoon and examined it closely. "I believe these small flowers on the handle are forget-me-nots. I recall seeing some very good examples of the blooms in your gardens, Mrs. Witton. Perhaps Miss Sarah would care to accompany me on a stroll about the grounds after breakfast. I could point them out to her."

"Kind of you to offer to indulge the child, my lord," said the bishop, "but Sarah has some reading to do... on the subject of impertinence." He looked at the girl in his own particular way.

Sarah's head sagged as she mumbled, "Yes, Father."

"Might I offer Faith and Marion as suitable deputies in her stead," Amanda said.

It was settled that the two young ladies would show Lord Rossiter over the grounds before he left to begin his research in the cathedral library. As the trio walked down the steps of the terrace, Rossiter looked up to the upper storey of the house and noticed a curtain drop back into place at one of the windows. He turned his attention to Faith and Marion, offering them each an arm for support.

The garden was of a formal design, split into four sections with paths crisscrossing each. Rossiter led the young ladies down the main gravel walk to a large fish pond that stood in the middle. As the young ladies bent to look into the pond his lordship glanced over his shoulder to the house.

"Odd, but I have the feeling that someone is watching us," he said.

"Oh, that is probably just Sarah," explained Faith, turning pink about the cheeks. "The dear girl takes the strangest notions into her head." She swallowed. "Sarah seems to think you're after the silver. Isn't that amusing?" She looked at Marion to get her out of her tangle.

"You see," Marion said in a confiding voice, "we Witton girls are all said to be just a little, er, different. It comes from having a bishop as a father."

"Marion!" Faith's eyes widened with shock. She pulled her sister to the side and whispered, "Such plain speaking before a guest is most unseemly, especially as he is only on slight terms with us."

Lord Rossiter led the young ladies over to a shaded bench. "I rather think I can sympathize with you. My esteemed parent was a fellow at Oxford. My academic achievements were always scrutinized thoroughly."

"It is a curious fact," Marion remarked, "that when one's parent is in a position of authority, one's own actions are inspected quite closely."

"That is true," Faith agreed. "Why, when poor Julia went for her first Season she had to guard her tongue and conduct herself in so saintly a fashion that she became bored with herself."

"Julia?" Rossiter gave Faith an intense look. "You mentioned the name Julia. Who might that be?"

Under such a fierce regard, Faith lapsed into silence. She blinked up at Rossiter, quaking at his harsh tone. She knew that his kindness wouldn't last long. There was a fearful glimmer in her eyes when she turned to Marion for help.

"Why, Julia is our sister," said Marion simply.

"Another one! Are you saying that Julia is Miss Witton?"

A look of tolerant amusement crept onto Marion's face as she enlightened his lordship. "Julia loathes being called Miss Witton. It is a constant reminder that she is the eldest unmarried daughter. One would never guess she is about to wed and settle into the staid life of a rector's wife, for she is full of fun and always ready for a lark. We are all a bit mischievous, though. It is our way of shaking off the fetters imposed upon us as children of a bishop. You must not mind our little foibles, my lord."

His lips compressed into a grim line. So, he thought. The well-bred Miss Witton and the shameless Julia were one and the same. The Bishop's eldest daughter had tricked him into thinking her an innocent, incapable of guile. A clandestine meeting with an officer? Ha! Was there nothing the vixen would not stoop to doing?

He gazed off into the distance at the summer-house and frowned. "Is that a gazebo I see?"

"Y-yes," Faith managed.

Rossiter looked down at the cautious expressions of his companions. His demeanour lightened and he smiled. "Would you show it to me? I've a fancy to see it."

The sisters exchanged a look, then Marion gave a tiny shrug and rose to her feet.

The summer-house proved to be a spacious affair that measured some twenty feet across. It stood banked by trees placed at a distance to provide shade, yet not obstruct the view of Lovers' Walk and the lush meadow at the garden's edge. There were chairs, tables and a Grecian couch arranged on the cool stone floor, showing that the place was well used by the family.

"How charming," commented Rossiter, glowering at the couch. In his mind he could envision the seduction of Miss Julia Witton by some inferior line officer. So the young bud was no doubt deflowered, wilting and losing her petals for any buck who passed in the night. He ought to have known.

Faith picked up a discarded book and tucked it away. "This is our favourite gathering place during the summer. We usually have tea here when the weather permits."

"Over there," Marion said, pointing toward the lane, "is Lovers' Walk. Many couples of a courting disposition have become victims of its legendary enchantment." She smiled in a disparaging way. "It is said that if a young man meets his lady-love at the Trysting Place—that's the large old oak at the other end of the lane—and they stroll together down Lovers' Walk, then within the month they shall be one. 'Tis nonsense, of course."

"It is not nonsense," Faith averred. "What about our brother John and Caroline? It worked for them. They've been married these three years or more."

"Oh, them." Marion made a dismissing motion with her hand. "They have loved each other since they were children."

Rossiter coughed gently, interrupting the two sisters. "I see I shall have to take care where I walk and with whom." He smiled at them.

Faith grinned back. "You needn't worry about me!" She put a hand to her mouth and looked stricken. A rosy blush tinted her cheeks. "What I mean to say is, you are the last man I would.... I mean..."

"We should be getting back," Marion inserted.

Rossiter escorted the young ladies through the garden to the house. He glanced up at the first floor. Again, a curtain dropped across one of the windows in the east wing.

He had much to think about as he made his way to his rooms. Before going to the cathedral he gave his valet, Minns, specific instructions concerning the sort of information he wanted the man to gather that day. As an afterthought, Rossiter scrawled out a note and handed it to him.

"I want it delivered to Miss Julia Witton when she is alone," his lordship said, as he walked out of his chamber door.

His activities that day kept him away from the house until it was time to dress for dinner. He returned to the manor, impatiently taking the steps two at a time. But when Cleeves opened the front doors to him, Lord Rossiter assumed a more languid demeanor.

That evening, the meal and the interminable time until the family retired dragged by with foot-tapping slowness. Mrs. Witton coaxed Faith and Marion into singing while she played the pianoforte. The finale, prior to retiring at ten o'clock, was a trembling effort on Faith's part to give a creditable performance on the harp. Before their mother could demand an encore, the girls escaped with the excuse of fatigue.

The bishop surprised his wife by offering to accompany her up to their suite of rooms, a departure from the normal custom. Seeing Amanda's startled look, he said, "Lord Rossiter desires to work undisturbed on his research."

"The man spends far too much time with flowers," Amanda remarked in an undertone.

Rossiter, left to his own devices, took up a chair in the library and waited.

As the pendulum clock in the hall struck the hour of eleven, the library door opened. The faint outline of a lady holding a candle appeared in the doorway. Julia entered attired in a dressing-gown and cap, which had a thick fall of lace shading her eyes.

She blew out her candle and placed it on a side table by the door. At her call Bounder trotted into the room and plopped down before the small fire in the grate.

Reluctant to come forward into the light of the single candelabrum next to Rossiter, she said, "I hope you'll forgive me for coming down in my night-clothes." She pulled at the top of her wrapper, even though aware that underneath she was properly attired in a day-dress. Still, she lingered by the doorway. "But I could not risk waking my sisters." She closed the door and began to advance toward him, then stopped. "Would you douse the candles? The bright light bothers my eyes."

Rossiter looked from the soft radiance of the candles back to Julia. A slight smile curled the corners of his mouth. "Ah, yes. I forgot. The measles, was it not?" He licked his fingertips and extinguished the flames. When he sat back in his chair, he found Julia comfortably ensconced on the sofa a good distance away from the dim light of the fire.

"I had not thought you a timid young woman, Miss Witton." He moved his chair to the sofa and sat down.

Her hand crept up to pull the lace further down over her eyes.

"A fetching cap, miss." His lips twitched. "I cannot recall ever seeing one with such an abundance of trimming. A new fashion here in Wells, is it?"

She peeked up at him from beneath the lacy curtain. "You, no doubt, have seen many bed caps in your time, sir. I do not usually wear one, but ever since this . . . this illness I have had to don it." She pulled at the ruffles until she felt more hidden. "Your note was quite cryptic, my lord. What is it that you wished to tell me?" she asked, hoping to move to safer ground.

"Why, nothing of extreme import. I merely enjoyed our chat last night and wished for another opportunity to further our acquaintance. Am I making you uncomfortable?"

"A little," she admitted. "My mother would have a severe attack of the vapours if she saw me thus. She taught her daughters how to properly receive a gentleman. I cannot recollect hearing her say that eleven at night was the appropriate hour for paying calls or that a dressing-gown was the correct attire for receiving a gentleman."

"There are occasions when we must transcend the proprieties." He looked down at the dog stretched out on the hearth-rug. "I see that you have brought a chaperone. Believe me, I fear for my life." Bounder yawned and licked his chops. He snuffled at Rossiter before going to sleep. The lord and the young lady smiled at each other, and settled in more comfortably.

"Truly, a remarkable cap, miss," he said, gazing lazily at her.

She watched the way his deep blue eye crinkled at the corner. "You may stop bamming me now, my lord. You think I look a shocking quiz, admit it."

An amused expression crossed his face. "I would be an odd guest indeed to agree with such an assessment." He tilted his head to the side in a considering fashion. "The cap is a quiz, but the lady in it is a puzzle which I intend to solve."

"Whatever can you mean, sir?" she remarked with the air of an innocent.

"My dear lady, the more I learn of you, the more perplexed I become."

Julia looked down at her hands. "I am just a simple country lass. There is nothing of a riddle about me."

"Is there not?" The flames in the grate reflected off his silver patch, making the look he sent her seem to blaze.

She moved back from the fire in his eyes. Yes, she mused, eyes. For the patch appeared to take on a life of its own, projecting Rossiter's emotions. It irked her to have to endure his fierce look. She had done nothing wrong. He was the one who met people by stealth.

There was just one man she would allow to cow her, and that man was her father, for he had the right to do so. He was the only one she would heed—the only one, that is, until Rossiter had come to visit. Now she understood something of what Faith felt when in the presence of this man. His stare made her think worriedly of past misdeeds.

She dared to square her shoulders and stare back at him. "What is it that you are fishing for, my lord?"

One corner of his mouth turned up. "Answers. I am fishing for answers to questions that perplex me." His expression began to close, like a curtain on a play. He stood, placing himself out of the firelight.

"If we are to speak of perplexities, sir, then answer me this—why are you here? What wondrous find brings you to Wells? My sisters tell me that you study flowers. They say you are on the trail of some specimen that has evaded your studies. Is this true?" Her disbelief was plain.

He looked down at her, examining her closely. "Most assuredly, miss, 'tis true."

Her sceptical expression stayed. "What is the name of this rare flower, sir?"

"Julia-is-a-riddle is the, ah, scientific term."

"An odd name."

"For an odd flower. One must study it to appreciate its fine beauty."

"Are you bamming me, milord? I've brothers, you see. I know there is honour among gentlemen, but not always between ladies and gentlemen. The truth, if you please."

Bounder raised his head. He looked about. A deep growl erupted from between his clenched teeth as his haunches went up and his head came down.

"There is someone out there," Julia whispered. She sat on the edge of the sofa and listened. A faint sound brought her to her feet. Quickly she moved toward one of the library windows. When she was halfway there, a foot came down on the hem of her dressing-gown, halting her in midstride. A great weight from behind caused her to pitch forward.

Lord Rossiter and Julia sprawled on the floor with a thud, her legs becoming entangled with his. She wriggled out of the precarious position.

"You tripped me!"

"How clumsy of me." He rolled back from her, then flicked a bit of dust from his sleeve.

"Why did you not want me to see who was out there?" she asked, tossing back the fall of lace from her eyes.

"What the devil!" He grabbed her chin and turned her face to the light. Touching the discoloration beneath her eye, he asked, "How did you come by this?"

She tried to pull away. "Unhand me, sir. I am marked enough." She found herself released, then pulled unceremoniously onto his lap. Her eyes flew wide open. "Are you mad! Release me, I say."

"My dear girl, now you've aroused my curiosity." He moved her chin with the tip of his long finger. A chuckle escaped him. The usual straight line of his lips lifted in one corner. "Do you indulge in fisticuffs, Miss Witton?"

"Only with deserving rogues who accost me in the moonlight, sir."

"Did you come by that eye defending your honour?"

She stiffened. She felt certain that he was laughing at her, and this irritated her to an irrational degree. She turned to confront him, her wide mouth set in a grim line.

"Just what do you imply? No man questions my honour, sirrah!" She balled up her hands.

He chuckled, and his warm breath fanned her neck. "Don't try to cozen me with talk of honour, my girl. I shall have the truth. The black eye?"

She glanced from side to side, as if weaving some elaborate fabrication in her mind. "A few nights ago," she began, "I was out strolling in the moonlight, woolgathering as is my wont. The night was so lovely that I scarcely heeded where I went. Well...I...I tripped. The next morning I awoke with this wretched eye."

"No doubt you were thinking of your heart's desire, your betrothed. I understand that love has the most curious effects upon those it smites." He smiled mockingly. "Your wedding is to be within a fortnight, I am told. How fortuitous. You and your beloved will soon be united in the lasting bonds of matrimony."

"Lasting bonds." Her voice had a leadened quality.

"The fellow must hold himself blessed above measure to have found such a prize. An honest, upright woman is a pearl beyond price."

His mocking words grated. In that moment she knew he was being as dishonest as she. It was not to be tolerated!

"You, sir, sit here very smug. Can you say that you have come to our home without guile? You look neither quite honest, nor quite dishonest. Are your intents and purposes so pure that you can judge another?" She recalled the text of the last sermon she had been compelled to read and flung its message in the haughty lord's face. "'He that is without sin, let him cast the first stone...'" she quoted.

Rossiter drew back in surprise. Surely in the face of his sarcasm this young lady should rightly have crumbled and confessed her darkest secret. "You think to rout me from my quest for the truth, hey, my girl?"

"Truth! What would a deceiver know of truth? Answer that if you dare."

He frowned at her. His thoughtful probing had turned into cap-pulling. And the hellcat was giving as good as she got. He dumped her off his lap and rose to tower over her.

"You have something that I want," he said. "I shall deal kindly with you if you'll give it without further fuss or commotion."

Julia clutched the top of her dressing-gown, choosing to misconstrue his meaning. "You wouldn't dare! Not in my father's own house." She delivered a wide-eyed look of shock.

"By heaven, I would if I thought 'twould get me what I'm after." He paused. "Tell me where it is!"

She drew herself up proudly. "I haven't a notion of what you are prattling on about. I suspect that you have been imbibing father's brandy." She scrambled up from the floor. "I hope your curiosity concerning me has been satisfied. Good night, sir!"

He grabbed her arm as she made to pass him. "Not entirely satisfied, miss." He pulled her closer to him. "Does Miss Witton bestow her favours upon every gentleman she's not engaged to, or merely those who stumble upon her in the moonlight?"

She gasped.

Rossiter held her closer still and tipped her chin up. He lowered his head. Their lips were inches from meeting.

"Don't you dare." She glared up at him.

He did dare, quite thoroughly. And not just once, but twice.

Julia stepped back, experiencing the uncertainty of diverging emotions. "What did you prove by taking those kisses?" she whispered. "That I am the wanton you think me? No. Only that you are the brute I thought you to be." She smiled in a confident way.

"Hellcat."

"Charlatan."

They glared at each other.

Bounder left off sniffing about the windowsill and came to stand by Julia. He growled.

"My chaperone reminds me that it is time to leave." She backed away from Rossiter and made for the door, whistling to Bounder as she ran for the stairs. Behind her, she left a candlestick and an inflamed peer, who vowed he would yet get what he wanted . . .

CHAPTER SEVEN

FROM THE FAR END of the meadow behind the manor house, Philippe Vodrey could see the garden and the summer-house as he held a spy-glass to his eye. He watched the movements of the Witton ladies with an intense interest. A small circle of red was left around his eye when he lowered his spy-glass. He drew back further into the underbrush and crawled to the place where he had stashed his gear.

A flask of wine, a basket of food and a blanket were tucked under a leafy bush a little distance from the edge of the meadow. He removed the stopper from the flask and downed a good portion of the wine. He found spying to be warm work. The day promised to get hotter and the prospect did not cheer him.

He blamed Trixie for his present uncomfortable duty. If the woman had kept her wits about her, the few she'd been blessed with, then he would have the pouch and be in France this very moment, receiving his rightful honours for completing the dangerous assignment for his country. But no, the woman had lost her small bit of courage, the courage he had taken great pains to imbue her with, and now he was reduced to snaking about like the lowliest of creatures.

It was all quite beneath him, the son of a nobleman in exile. Quibbling with Napoleon's agent had been demeaning, wooing Trixie had been loathsome, but this skulking about was the most lowering task of all. He was unconcerned about the necessity of killing an English agent or two. Doing that sort of thing troubled him little. If he could be restored the position, titles and lands that were once his by right, then he would do what was required of him.

A rustling in the undergrowth caught his attention. He pulled out his pocket pistol and crouched in readiness.

"Mr. Day," a hoarse voice whispered. "Mr. Day? Mr. Day!"

Philippe shook his head in disgust. That he, a member of the noble house of Vodrey, should be reduced to using a fool as a henchman was scarcely to be endured. He was thankful that the brainless mass of muscle knew him only by a false name. Who knew what information the fool might thoughtlessly give away?

Clicking his fingers, Philippe signalled the man. The burly fellow thrashed about in the bushes until he found Philippe's hiding place.

"You fool," Philippe whispered, "do you want to alert all those up at the house that I am here? Why not have the butler, Cleeves, announce me? *Mon dieu*, I should have left you in London. Now, what has brought you thrashing in here?"

The large man looked down at the ground, shamefaced, and shuffled his feet back and forth. "I came to tell you that Silverpatch just returned to the manor house."

"Where did he go and what did he do while he was gone?"

"I followed him as you told me to do. He went to the cathedral. Stayed inside the bookroom there for nigh on three hours. Minns, that valet of his, came and went regular like." The man put his weight on one foot, brushing the ground with the toe of his other boot. "I couldn't watch 'em both. You said to watch Silverpatch, so I did."

"I pray, Stokes, that you did not stand outside the library waiting all that time for Silverpatch, as you call him."

"Nah, I waited outside the cathedral, watching the door he went in—real careful like."

Philippe sputtered with anger. "Idiot! There are a dozen or more exits from the cathedral. He could have slipped out whenever he chose."

"Mayhap you should have Bateman watch 'im and let me keep an eye on the lady and her maid. Bateman is much better at following than me. I am a good guard."

Philippe rubbed his temple and grimaced. "Go back to the inn, then, and guard the women. Tell Bateman to join me here. And, Stokes, try not to be seen by anyone from the manor house."

Stokes ambled off through the woods. Philippe winced as his henchman tramped noisily over dry twigs and branches. The necessity of doing away with the fellow appealed to Philippe. He would tend to the job himself, just as soon as he had the pouch.

With these pleasant thoughts in his head, Philippe crawled back to the edge of the meadow and peered across to the manor grounds. He raised the spy-glass to his eye and watched.

In the summer-house, Amanda sat with her three younger daughters. Sarah had draped herself along the Grecian couch, Amanda and Faith sat close to each other doing needlework, and Marion, gazing at the pages of a book, leaned against the railing a little distance from the others.

"What do you mean, Faith," Amanda demanded, "by saying you cannot like him? Lord Rossiter is an eligible, well-bred gentleman."

"Yes, Mama," Faith replied. "But eligible or no, the man makes me uneasy." She squirmed on her chair.

"Why, my dear child," Amanda replied, "anyone can see that you have a stirring of emotions when you are near his lordship. You are so overcome that you can scarcely keep your seat. I am sure that the very sight of him makes you quiver—a clear indication of your affection for him."

"Mama! The man frightens me." Faith fanned herself. "He has the look of a pirate, what with that patch and all."

"Such a romantic visage he has! It is no wonder you are so taken with him." Amanda held her hand over her heart and sighed.

"Mama!" Faith wailed.

"I daresay, dear Mama," Marion remarked as she moved closer and placed her hand on her mother's shoulder, "that Faith is trying to tell you that she does not wish for a lasting connection with Lord Rossiter."

"Nonsense," Amanda stated. "Faith is too young to know what she wants."

"Just a moment ago you were telling me that I was old enough to be considering marriage quite seriously." Faith looked at her mother in confusion.

Amanda smoothed her gown. "You are old enough, nay, past the age to marry, but still young enough to need the wise counsel of your mother to guide you in choosing the man you should wed. Why, at the age of seventeen I married your father. The next year, your eldest brother, John, was born. I promised myself that my own daughters would know such happiness, but look at you. Here's Marion just finished a successful Season with many offers, yet would she have any of the gentlemen who begged for her hand? No! And you, Faith, in your twenty-first year and still a spinster. As for your sister, Julia . . . Well! At last, at four-and-twenty, she is to be wed. Where have I failed? What have I done that Providence should strike such a blow?"

"Now, Mama," Marion said, taking Faith's fan and waving it before her mother's face, "you do not want to overset yourself and bring about a spasm. We admit to being the most wretched daughters ever to curse a mother. Our fickle hearts have made us all old maids—a fitting punishment for such waywardness."

"Do not try to soothe me with empty words," Amanda said. "It is my duty as your mother to see that you are wed. It is your duty as my daughters to marry—early and well."

"Yes, Mama," Faith and Marion said together.

"Now, Faith, about Lord Rossiter—" Amanda began.

"Shh," Marion cautioned, "he's coming."

His lordship strolled up the gravel path to the summer-house. "Dear lady," he said, turning to Amanda, "I never tire of looking at your lovely blooms." He smiled at the young ladies in his cool way. "With such comely daughters, ma'am, your gardens can hardly compare. Ah, the beauties of nature. Fascinating!"

"How do your studies fare?" Amanda asked.

"My research goes slowly, ma'am. Unearthing bits of information takes time. How refreshing to come to this cool, quiet place after a day of rummaging through dusty books."

"I daresay," Sarah spoke up, "that anything would look better than a room full of books." She looked at him queerly. "Do you enjoy reading all day?"

Marion went over to sit next to Sarah on the couch, pushing the girl's feet down so that she was forced to sit up. Jabbing her elbow into Sarah's ribs, Marion motioned her to hush.

"As pleasing as it is to feast one's gaze on the lovely countenance of your three daughters," Rossiter said in his flowery way that held more than a hint of play-acting, "I am most desirous of making the acquaintance of Miss

Witton, your eldest daughter. When might I be granted that opportunity? I sense that this bouquet of young buds is incomplete without her."

Amanda shifted uncomfortably. "This illness is most precarious, my lord. One doesn't know from one day to the next how much better she will look—ah, feel."

"I understand that Miss Witton's betrothed is due to arrive any day." Rossiter strolled over to the railing and leaned against one of the stone columns that supported the roof. "I assume this is an engagement of long standing?"

"Too long," Sarah muttered.

"Not too long," Amanda said, fanning herself. "Merely a few months' time."

"Miss Witton must be anxious for her nuptials," Rossiter commented, as he polished his quizzing-glass on the sleeve of his coat.

"Anxious? Yes," Marion replied, "she is quite anxious." Then in a voice that only Sarah heard, she murmured, "Anxious to be rid of Oglesby."

Amanda fanned herself more briskly. "You must know that brides-to-be have the fidgets over the merest nothing."

"That's Mr. Oglesby," Sarah whispered, "the merest nothing." She owed the present continuance of her life to the distance of Rossiter from where she sat. If her mother had thought his lordship had heard her, Sarah would have been banished to her room forever. As it was, she could only guess at how many pages she would be required to read.

"This engagement has the ring of a love match, ma'am."

"Why, yes, it is," affirmed Amanda. "I knew Mr. Oglesby when he was a child. When he wrote to ask for Julia's hand I was delighted. And she, quite taken aback by his offer, consented after a . . . a brief time of reflection."

The Witton girls exchanged looks. They knew that Julia had complied with their mother's wishes concerning Mr. Oglesby only after a long struggle of wills. As for being quite taken, Julia had taken to her bed suffering a severe case of the dismals. The thought of an arranged marriage to a man she had never met was truly a dampening one.

Rossiter raised his polished glass toward the gardens. "Pray tell, could that, ah, sprig of fashion approaching be the much awaited bridegroom?" The ladies turned to gaze in the direction that Rossiter's quizzing-glass pointed.

Amanda perked up in her chair and beamed brightly. Her daughters sank down in their seats with a moan.

Along the gravel path ambled a darkly dressed scare-crow of a man. As Atley Oglesby came nearer, Rossiter brought his glass up to view the rector. His lordship could be forgiven if his mouth dropped open. Mr. Oglesby was a sight to behold.

The rector's gait as he walked toward them hardly al-lowed for the bending of his knees. He gave the appear-ance of being tall, but his height was merely average. It was his thin form that misled the eye. The leggings he wore ac-centuated his spindle-shanked aspect.

"I am here," Mr. Oglesby proclaimed. He moved his stiff neck slightly to view the company before him. The elevation of his chin had nothing to do with the height of his shirt points, which were moderate. It was his own sense of importance that caused the exaggerated posture.

"What the deuce," muttered Rossiter, mesmerized by the man before him.

"Mr. Oglesby," Amanda murmured, her eyes upon the oily locks of the fine, pale head of hair that was lowered before her. She recalled his cherubic looks as a youth and repressed a sigh. The rector now appeared to have adopted a new coiffure for the wedding. His thin hair was arranged flat to his head and the curled ends framed his face.

"At least his face is not so mottled with spots as before," whispered Marion to Sarah.

"The spots will come out the moment he sees Julia," Sarah retorted under her breath.

At last Mr. Oglesby straightened from paying homage to the bishop's lady. "Mother Witton," he said, looking down his pinched nose at her, then he puckered his thin lips and leaned forward. But his sharp nose brushed her cheek before his lips could. "I hope that as a soon-to-be member of the family you will permit such liberties." His voice was as thin as his person.

Calling upon her talents as a hostess, Amanda made the rector known to the gentleman who stood staring at him.

Rossiter's eyes sparkled as he gazed at the rector. "So, you're Miss Witton's betrothed."

"I have that honour, my lord," replied Atley Oglesby, as he looked down along his nose in Rossiter's direction. His gangly, large-knuckled hands rested upon his knees as he sat down on a chair. "I am most eager to see her. Is she away from home visiting in the neighbourhood, Mother Witton?" The rector craned his head toward where Amanda had taken a seat upon the couch with her two daughters.

Amanda's hands fluttered helplessly. His direct question about Julia left her not knowing quite how to respond. This was not at all what she had planned.

"Julia is indisposed today, Mr. Oglesby," Marion said. "She has been ill for a number of days now."

The rector's nostrils flared, but the rest of his face remained passive. "I pray that it is not a serious indisposition. I long to see her." Not an ounce of longing carried in his voice.

In the face of this tepid passion, Rossiter thrust himself back into the conversation. "We are told that she is languishing for the sight of you, sir. No doubt her recovery will be swift now that you have arrived."

The rector's hands began to move over his knees in a massaging manner, as if his thoughts were elsewhere. His Adam's apple bobbed up and down along his elongated neck. "I await the moment of our meeting with the greatest anticipation."

"Julia is counting the days until the wedding," Amanda happily offered. She neglected to say that Julia marked off each day with an angry-looking blot of ink.

"Twelve days." Oglesby wiped his damp hands together and turned in Amanda's direction. "Pray excuse me, but I wish to retire. My journey was quite long. I hope my room is a goodly distance from Miss Witton's. My uncle, the Bishop of Durham, thought that all the proprieties should be observed."

Amanda stared quizzically at the rector, wondering what sort of impropriety such a stiff-necked bridegroom would take with her daughter. Her mind began to picture Mr. Oglesby as the impatient lover. But the exercise proved to be most improper and she gave up the ludicrous feat.

With a slight blush on her cheeks, Amanda said, "I daresay you need a long rest. In your honour, tomorrow we shall dine in state. I am sure that Julia will be coming down by then."

The rector unbent from his chair and got to his feet. He bowed over Mrs. Witton's hand. Then he quit the summer-house as if leaving the presence of royalty, scraping and bowing as he backed out.

Mr. Oglesby was scarcely out of sight when Marion rounded on her mother. "Mama, for pity sake, allow Julia to ask for a release from her promise."

"This is not a topic for discussion, especially before our guest." Amanda pinched Marion on the arm as she glanced in Rossiter's direction.

"Mama, we must speak," Marion murmured.

Amanda rose. "Not now, my dear. It is time that we dress for dinner. You mustn't keep Betty waiting. She scolds so. Besides, your father will be home shortly." Leaving this vague threat hanging over them, she started for the gravel path, then looked back as Rossiter moved closer to her daughters. "Come, girls."

The young ladies dipped a curtsey to his lordship and left to follow Amanda. As they mounted the main staircase in the house, Faith and Marion surrounded their mother and made a verbal assault.

"Mama," Faith whispered so the servants would not hear, "I have never questioned your and Father's judgment before, but now I must. I cannot like Mr. Oglesby for Julia. He is not at all the sort of man she would be happy with. I had believed he would improve upon better acquaintance, but he has not."

"You needn't like Mr. Oglesby," Amanda retorted. "As long as Julia is satisfied with him."

"But is she?" Sarah looked at her mother accusingly. "I do not recall that she had much choice in the matter. Mama, the man is a bore."

"Then Julia will balance their life together nicely, for she has no notion of decorum." Amanda turned up the stairs to the west wing. "It would displease me to have to inform your father that his children were meddling in concerns that are better left to wiser heads. I am sure that Mr. Hobson's tomes have much in them on the duty of children to their parents."

"I don't care a fig if I must read a hundred pages," Sarah stated. "I will have my say."

Faith laid a restraining hand upon her younger sister's arm. "Have a care," she advised in a low voice.

"But we are speaking of our sister's happiness," protested Sarah.

"Do not speak to me of Julia's happiness when you know so little of the matter." With that, Amanda marched up to her rooms.

"Marion, what's to be done?" Faith's gentle countenance was wrinkled with worry.

A thoughtful look stole over Marion's face. "What we need is some other eligible to whisk Julia out from under Mr. Oglesby's sharp nose. I believe Mama is only concerned that our sister marry. Whom she marries is merely incidental."

Faith frowned. "Yes, but who?":

Marion considered for a moment. "There is an eligible staying with us. Do *you* want to wed Lord Rossiter?" When Faith's cheeks whitened, Marion said, "Then he shall be for Julia."

Back in the summer-house, Rossiter appeared to be in no hurry to change his raiment for dinner. He was content to remain, enjoying the afternoon sun. The light danced upon his face, causing the silver patch to come to life. It seemed to glow with a deep, burning determination. A devilish smile curled the corners of his mouth as he said, "Oglesby be damned!"

CHAPTER EIGHT

THE PEACE OF THE MANOR HOUSE in its early-morning slumber was slightly discomposed when the pendulum of the hall clock struck the hour of five. As the last chime faded into the grey dimness of the dawn, someone stealthily moved up the flight of stairs to the west wing. Along the dark corridor the robed figure crept, seeming to know the placement of the furniture arranged against the walls. At the door leading into the Red Rooms, the intruder entered without pause.

The antechamber was dark. The heavy damask drapery hanging over the windows effectively kept all light from entering the small room. Yet the intruder navigated around the furniture with ease.

Upon reaching the door to the dressing-room, the trespasser placed an ear to it. A slight squeak was emitted by the hinges as the door opened inward.

The dressing-room lay in deep darkness. As the drapes were carefully drawn back, the rings made a faint clicking noise. A bit of grey light entered the room. The slim figure stood in silhouette against the window and listened. Perceiving no sound, the intruder moved to the chair before the dressing-table, then froze as the chair scraped the floor. The creak of a floorboard startled the trespasser, who turned and dashed toward the door leading out. Another, much larger, figure leaped across the pale patch of light coming from the window.

Rossiter grasped the slender figure in an ancient wrestling hold. He tossed his thrashing victim back against the wall and raised his fist, ready to deliver a stunning blow.

"Julia!" He stepped away from her, still holding her by the shoulder. "What the devil are you doing here?"

"What?" she asked faintly. "Where am I? Lord Rossiter, why are you forever grabbing me? Really, sir, my mother shall hear of this!" She tried to pull out of his grasp.

"And what would your upright mother say if she were told I found her eldest daughter wandering about in my rooms before the break of day?"

"Your rooms? These are your rooms? Oh, dear! I've done it again." Julia put a hand to her head. "You see, I sometimes walk in my sleep. I am a night-rambler."

"Are you now?" Rossiter gazed at her in an interested fashion. "How very disconcerting for the worthy Mr. Oglesby. He may wake one morning to find his sweet bride has wandered off."

Julia looked closely at the man who continued to hold her to the wall with his hands on either side of her body. His patch had been removed and an apparently useful, unscarred blue eye was looking back at her.

"Is it glass?" She leaned closer to see.

He laughed light-heartedly. "No."

She touched the corner of his eye. "There is nothing wrong. Why do you hide it?"

Rossiter took her hand from his eye. "I am the questioner here, if you will recall. You were about to explain this curious habit of night rambling."

"Please, keep your voice down," Julia whispered. "Mama has ears that hear through walls."

"I shall begin to shout the house down if you continue to evade my questions."

"Lord Rossiter, I truly suspect your sanity. First you demanded I meet you in my father's library, where you accosted me and treated me like a strumpet..." She looked down at the compromising position they were in. "And now, here you are doing it again. I believe you've become unhinged, sir."

"And I believe you are the most adept liar I have ever had the misfortune to meet, and you a bishop's daughter."

"I, a liar?" She drew herself up, taking umbrage at his words. They might be true, but nevertheless, the words could not be allowed to pass unchallenged. "Are you calling the daughter of a bishop a liar?" She glared at him. "Sir, I have told you that I chanced into your rooms by the caprice of Fate. I beg your pardon for disturbing your slumber. If you hurry back to bed, perhaps you'll not lose too much sleep."

He looked at her hair tumbling about her shoulders. There was no cap now hiding her thick, soft curls. Her hair looked quite touchable.

"Ah, 'to sleep, perchance to dream, ay, there's the rub.' No cap tonight, hey?" He wound a light brown curl about his fingers. "Did you know, Miss Witton, that I find you delectable?" he asked in an off-handed manner. "I particularly find your mouth most interesting."

Julia squirmed as he stepped nearer. "Let me go, sir, or I swear I shall do you an injury."

He moved away, smiling at her. "'Tis a shame to waste a delightful woman on a walking-stick parson. I do not believe that you and Oglesby will suit. That pulpit-thumper would not know what to do with a liar."

"You needn't be insulting. Besides, I did not ask for your opinion of Mr. Oglesby." She looked at him in a considering way. "If you don't think I came here while walking in my sleep, then what, in heaven's name, do you think brought me here?''

His gaze searched her face. An ironic smile curled his lips. "If I were a great conceited ass, I would say that a desire to see me privately brought you here. But my conceits are not so great and I doubt that you would want to bed with a scarred old soldier. So I must ask myself, if you did not come here to compromise me, then what could have lured you into my rooms? Mayhap you were looking for something else besides pleasure and company. Something of value..." He looked about.

She allowed him to go no further in his thinking as she threw herself into his arms. "Milord, I cannot deny it any longer. You have my heart," she proclaimed dramatically. "I have tried to stay away, but something drew me here to...to you!" She grabbed the front of his dressing-gown and kissed him. Then she pushed away, as if scorched, and stumbled back. "I...I am pledged to another. I have no right to be here. This is wrong!" She turned away. Out of the corner of her downcast eyes, she looked to see his reaction to her performance.

His brows rose in surprise. He moved to stand close behind her. "I am...honoured by your confession." An odd catch in his voice tripped his words. He hid his amused smile in her hair as he held her close to him.

A loud tap at the antechamber door made Julia spring from him. The tapping continued, then Amanda Witton's voice called softly, "Lord Rossiter? Lord Rossiter? Are you awake, milord?"

"Mama," Julia exclaimed in a fierce whisper. She glanced about, then made for the clothes-press.

Rossiter grabbed her arm before she could squeeze in with his coats. "Let us face her together and confess all."

"Are you mad?" She pried at his fingers on her arm. "This is worse than eloping. Let me go!"

"Hide if you must, my dear, but not among my coats, if you please."

"Lord Rossiter," Amanda said through the door, "I hear voices. Are you awake?"

Julia darted for the bedchamber. A deep chuckle followed her as she plunged into the dark room. In a low voice she begged him to hush.

Carefully closing the door after her, he began to set the stage for his part of the performance. He undid the fastenings of his dressing-gown, letting it hang open, knowing that would surely avert Mrs. Witton's eyes. Then he rumpled his dark hair and assumed the aspect of one just having awakened. He looked back at the bedchamber door and smiled.

In the hall, Amanda was gathering the courage to enter his lordship's chambers. When she heard the stumbling footsteps coming closer to the door, she allowed her righteous indignation to cool. A great bumping followed by a curse heralded Lord Rossiter's arrival. Amanda adjusted her lacy cap and smoothed her concealing wrapper.

The door to the antechamber was inched open. "Ma'am?" Rossiter asked in a sleepy voice.

"I do beg your pardon, my lord, but I woke and heard voices coming from your rooms." She paused and blushed at the thoughts that were flitting through her head. "Is there something you would like to tell me, sir?" After all, she reasoned, as the wife of the bishop she could not allow trifling with the maids under her own roof. It was not seemly.

Rossiter held his hand over his left eye, in place of the patch, and thrust his head through the opening of the door. Amanda gasped and stepped back.

"Where... where is your patch?"

He yawned. "It must have fallen off. I am the one who should beg your pardon, ma'am. Since my time in the army I have been prone to speaking in my slumbers. The fighting stays with me. If I've alarmed you, pray forgive me."

"Oh, of course. The war..." Amanda's voice died away on her unspoken thoughts. Polite ladies did not discuss the war with gentlemen. Her hand crept up to her throat as she muttered her regrets for waking him. Backing away, Amanda turned and retreated down the corridor to rejoin the bishop in their bedchamber.

The bishop shivered when Amanda climbed back into bed. "Mandy, your feet are cold. Where have you been?"

"Oh, Emory, the war does such terrible things. I wonder where Lucian is now."

The bishop wrapped his arm about her and held her close. He whispered quiet words of comfort until Amanda drifted off to sleep.

Back in the Red Rooms, Rossiter, not at all sleepy, entered his bedchamber. "Julia? Come out, come out wherever you are," he whispered.

The bed curtains parted. Julia peered out and looked this way and that, then stepped down. She moved swiftly away from the disreputable piece of furniture.

"Damnation, girl, your mother would have fainted dead away if she'd caught you in there. What the devil made you choose that place to hide?"

"'Tis the last place Mama would have looked. The fear of seeing what she thinks she'd see if she looked would keep her from peeking behind the bed curtains."

He smiled as he nodded his head. "Yes, she fairly flew back to her rooms when she thought that she might see my eye, or what she imagined was left of it." He crossed to the table beside the bed and lit a candle, then picked up the patch by its silken cords. He twirled the cord on and off his finger as he watched Julia.

"Mama is not really a coward. She simply prefers to avoid what she imagines will be unpleasant. It gave me quite a start to discover that the patch is a ruse." She looked at him with a questioning expression. He began to put the patch back in place. "You needn't wear that on my account. You appear rather agreeable without it—less fierce looking."

"Oh?" One eyebrow came up as he gave her a quizzical stare. But he removed the patch and held it.

"I think you go to a great deal of trouble to hide behind the thing." She saw him smile. "You enjoy wearing that patch, don't you?"

"It serves its purpose."

"Which is?"

His smile widened into a full, unaffected one. He looked quite different, much more approachable. "To frighten away eager young ladies and their mamas."

"And to keep the rest of humankind at a distance," she added.

His gaze moved slowly over her face. "Not all of humankind. Most assuredly not all."

"You rogue," she murmured.

He bowed in acknowledgement. "I am whatever you will," he replied, moving close to her. She backed away from him until she was stopped by a large chest resting next to the wall. "Your mother interrupted a most interesting conversation. You were saying something about your heart..."

She took a ragged breath and put her hand to her chest. The pounding beneath her fingers felt as if she had just run up a hill. She looked at him in a bemused way. How could Faith malign the man as she did? He was charming.

"What about my heart?" she asked, her tone warm and low.

"You were saying I had possession of it. Then, as I recollect, you threw yourself in my arms and kissed me." He sighed. "A pity your mama came along just as I was being carried away by your passionate avowal. We shall have to rectify that."

Slipping away from him along the edge of the chest, she asked, "How?"

"Come now, my dear girl, the time for maidenly modesty is long passed. A lady who hides in a gentleman's bed can surely trust that gentleman with her virtue."

"That is a shabby sort of logic. I would wager many maids have fallen because of it."

"Don't you trust me?" he asked with some surprise.

"Lord Rossiter, a man of your mercurial temperament and, ah, passions shouldn't ask such questions." She smiled. "My answer might inflame you. Surely I have maddened you enough during our brief acquaintance."

He smiled back at her. "Acquaintance, Julia? That is far too tame a word for the moments we've spent together. With such a thorough knowledge of one another, I feel at ease using your name. You might use mine—it's Thomas."

"Sir, you forget that I am to be married!"

"No, I never forget that. I daresay you forget, much to my everlasting delight. But let us not get to wrangling with each other. There are so many more pleasant things to do." At her gasp he stepped away from her and leaned against the wall, folding his arms over his chest. He knew that he should behave as a gentleman. Yet, he felt far from gentlemanly in her presence. "It is important that you trust me, my dear. For I believe you have something that belongs to me."

She grinned. "Your heart?"

He shook his head. "You keep playing games. But the time I can spare for games is coming to an end. Time is becoming my enemy."

Julia moved restlessly away. Time was her enemy, too. Yet, she could not bring herself to wholly trust this man regardless of his earnest demeanour. He was as Sarah said—smoky. Even though she felt an urge to speak of the pouch, she knew she must remain silent until she learned more.

"Your words have the sound of a desperate man, milord. But I have nothing you could possibly want."

A slow grin spread across Thomas's face. The corner of his lips curled up in a lopsided fashion. He pushed away from the wall and moved closer to her. "Do you know what happens to a bishop's daughter who lies?" He twirled the patch by the end of its cord. "A one-eyed demon swoops down on her and carries her off to his lair."

"I don't suppose they live happily ever after, do they? A bishop's daughter rarely gets along with a demon."

"Ah, but when they do get along . . ." His smile finished the sentence for him. He glanced over at his bed. A wistful sigh escaped him.

"Someone ought to knock you down," she stated.

"Won't the sanctimonious Atley Oglesby oblige you?"

"Don't be ridiculous!" She cast him an angry look. Why was he always bringing Oglesby into their conversations? She pushed past him and stormed out of the bedchamber. A soft chuckle from behind nearly caused her to slam the door, but she remembered her mother sleeping down the hall and softly crept back to her room.

At the gentle closing of the door, Rossiter entered the dressing-room. He stood surveying its contents, his hands resting on his hips. His blue eyes narrowed thoughtfully as he gazed at the chair pulled toward the clothes-press. He moved to the chair and positioned it before the doors of the press, then climbed up. His hand brushed along the top. At the feel of something flat and made of leather, he smiled.

ABOUT TWO MILES from the manor house, in a vale near Wookey Hole, stood an old inn. After Wookey Hole was discovered some local had thought to make his fortune from the crowds that would come to view the famous caves. His enterprising inn had long since been abandoned as a folly. But at present, the out-of-the-way place was being used. Whiffs of smoke made their way up the chimney and floated over the surrounding grassy hills.

A burly man, his shirt-sleeves rolled up and his plain jerkin soiled, came out of the weathered front door. Stokes, Philippe Vodrey's henchman, carried a bucket down the path toward the stream beyond the outbuildings. After filling the bucket, he lumbered back to the inn.

As he entered the hostelry by the kitchen door, a scathing voice greeted him. "*Mon dieu!* Where is my breakfast, you lazy slug?"

"I had to fetch water for the ladies," Stokes mumbled by way of an explanation.

"You are not their lackey, you're mine!" Philippe pushed Stokes toward the fireplace. "Those women are prisoners, not guests. Prepare my food, then get over to the manor house. See that you are hired for the day at the stables. Servants hear things. I want you to be my ears at the manor." Vodrey went into the taproom and drew a tankard of ale from the new keg perched upon the bar.

A door at the top of the stairs opened, and light footsteps could be heard descending the rickety steps. Marie, the maid, entered the taproom and stopped short at the sight of Philippe. Watching him, she called out, "Monsieur Stokes, is Madam's water ready?"

Stokes entered and looked down at the bucket he still held, then at the empty kettle on the hob. "Sorry, miss. Orders." He glanced at Philippe.

With a jerk of his head, Philippe motioned Stokes out. "My breakfast, dolt. I shall handle things here." His gaze moved over Marie.

Shuffling out the door, Stokes left the two alone.

Philippe flashed a handsome smile. "I have been wanting to talk to you, Marie. You have been much upon my mind of late. Tell me, do you ever find yourself thinking of me?"

Marie gave him a disquieted look, then lowered her eyes. "I . . . I am sure *madam* would be most displeased if I had thoughts of you."

"Forget *madam*. This is between you and me."

"But there can never be anything between us."

He grinned. "You were wrong. There could be much passion. And I could be most generous. I am offering you my protection, chère Marie."

"But *madam* is your love."

"She knows nothing of real love. The romantic fool won't even allow me to kiss her full on the lips. I shall tell you something, *chérie*. *Madam* is afraid of the warm passion two people can share. But you are different."

She backed away from his look. "*Madam* will be wondering what keeps me from attending her. I must go."

"Your mistress won't trouble herself to stir from bed before noon. There is no one about to disturb us." He began to ease out of his coat.

"Marie!" Trixie called from the top of the stairs. "Come here at once."

The maid backed to the door. "Coming, *madam*!" She darted out of the taproom and up the stairs.

"Where have you been?" Trixie demanded, as Marie entered the shabby little chamber. "Never mind your long-winded tales. Where is my water? You know I cannot dress until I have washed in rose-scented water."

"The man Stokes must make the breakfast of that one before he can heat your water."

A pout appeared on Trixie's pretty lips. "Philippe has become quite rude since we have come here. Why, by the way he behaves one would think we were prisoners. But that's nonsense! My stepbrother has the papers and is long gone by now."

"If that is so, then why does this one stay here? He will go wherever the papers go."

"He told me we were waiting for a suitable transport to take us to France. He is worried that Rossiter will come after us, so we must hide here for a time." Trixie looked about the room and shuddered. "Philippe regrets the hardship, but every great love must pass through the fiery realms before reaching its true fulfilment. It is all part of being in love."

The maid snorted with Gallic disdain. "*Madam*, I tell you, we must get away. That Philippe is evil. He holds you as a tool against your brother. It was he who saw to it that I went into service for you. He was the one who made your husband seem ridiculous and undesirable. He has filled your head with romantic notions, and you have believed him."

Trixie's eyes filled with tears. "You say those cruel things because you are jealous. Every woman envies what I have—a pure, undefiled love. My Philippe is a fine gentleman incapable of lust or base acts of the flesh."

Marie sighed and began to mumble a string of prayers.

CHAPTER NINE

THE DINNER GONG RANG that evening at the precise time it always did. At its ringing, the bishop's daughters began to assemble to go downstairs together. Each inspected the other, for it would not do to show themselves before their parents and guests presenting a less-than-perfect appearance. To this end, Julia applied an extra coating of rice powder over the yellowish bruise under her eye.

Sarah and Marion, in white gowns of fine muslin, teased each other about who among them looked the most stylish. Dressed in pale lilac, Faith went about settling the argument in her gentle way.

For a reason known only to herself, Julia had taken great pains to look her best. Her soft yellow satin gown fell in lovely folds, swaying when she moved. A row of spangles glimmered beneath her bodice and at the edge of her small puffed sleeves.

"Don't you look the smart," Sarah observed as she walked around Julia.

Drawing her Norwich shawl about her and moving toward the door, Julia said, "Come along, or else we shall keep Father waiting."

The Witton girls made quite a picture as they descended the main staircase together. Their kinship was evident in their mannerisms, features and smiles. They all wore the wide, engaging smile that seemed to be the hallmark of the bishop's daughters. It was generally held that the young Witton ladies were among the loveliest in the county.

Amanda beamed when her daughters entered the drawing-room. She took Julia over to Lord Rossiter to formally introduce the pair. Then she left them to pry Mr. Oglesby from the bishop's side.

Rossiter bowed low after the young lady was presented to him and murmured. "Julia?"

"You, sir, may address me as Miss Witton." She rose from her curtsey, smiling as if nothing untoward was happening. "We have not met before, remember?" The memory of kissing him and of the man he was without the patch flitted through her mind. But she shook it away.

Amanda returned with the eager rector in tow. "And here is dear Mr. Oglesby, at last. I daresay you two would like a moment alone. Lord Rossiter, do come see what Faith has done with the bunch of flowers she picked this morning." She steered his lordship over to a vase on a side table.

"Well, Mr. Oglesby." Julia swallowed hard. "I see you have arrived." A pity, she mused, as she watched him take her hand and plant a kiss on the back of it, leaving a wet mark where his lips had been.

"My dear, dear Miss Witton, only my duties to my parish and my uncle, the Bishop of Durham, could keep me from joining you sooner." He lowered his voice. "I have longed to see you."

The smile faded from her lips. "The anticipation of seeing *you* has kept me awake at night," she admitted, with a distasteful shudder.

A light seemed to brighten Oglesby's pale eyes. "Has it been thus with you also? I will only say that I am counting the hours that bring me closer to making you my bride."

Julia glanced from Oglesby over to Rossiter. His gaze travelled smoothly from Faith to Julia. They exchanged a look of understanding. Then the silver patch seemed to wink at her. He turned back to Faith and took up their conversation again, but his gaze continued to drift over to the betrothed couple from time to time.

Mrs. Witton's glance darted back and forth between the two couples. "They do make a fine-looking pair." She sighed.

The bishop, sitting next to her sipping his cordial, raised his brows. "Who?"

"Faith and—" Amanda lowered her voice "—Lord Rossiter."

A stern look came to the bishop's face. "Forget that match, my dear. She is afraid of him and he is bored with her."

"Perhaps Marion should chat with his lordship for a time."

"Amanda..."

The tone of the bishop's voice caused his wife to utter a meek, "Yes, dear." Then she brightened. "I do look forward to seeing Julia settled at last."

"You and Mr. Oglesby seem to be the only ones who do."

A defensive look came over Amanda's face. "If that is so, then it is only because Julia is suffering from the natural qualms which every bride has before her wedding."

"I believe that her qualm is called doubt."

"Doubt? Nonsense! What Julia is doing is right. How can marrying a rector, whose uncle is a bishop of one of the finest sees in the kingdom, be wrong? How can one construe marrying a man of the Church to be wrong? He is all that he should be."

The Bishop was silent for a moment. "Remind me, my dear, to take a greater part in the choosing of our next daughter's husband."

At that moment, Cleeves entered the drawing-room to announce dinner. The bishop gave his wife a closed look. Casting him a puzzled glance, Amanda went about her duties as hostess. She had just taken Lord Rossiter's arm to lead the others into dinner, when the doors of the drawing-room opened again.

Upon the threshold stood Harry, devoid of his recent travel stains and nicely attired in his regimentals. A playful smile danced across his face. "I most humbly beg your forgiveness, ma'am, for coming to you when you've guests," he said, walking toward Amanda. He got no further in his prepared speech. The Witton girls dropped all claim to decorum and rushed to his side. They greeted him as if he had been away an age.

Rossiter watched the exchange of greetings closely. It was difficult to tell which of the four sisters was happiest to see their friend and neighbour. They all appeared to share equally in the joy of his arrival, a joy noticeably lacking in their reception of Mr. Oglesby.

The different manner in which each sister behaved toward the major greatly interested his lordship. Sarah, who reached Harry first, socked him on his good arm and said she knew he would not fail them. Faith seemed to step out of herself as she engaged in a quick exchange of friendly banter with him. Yet Marion, a quick-witted girl, looked to be tongue-tied, almost shy. She gave Harry a brief hug, but that was all. The one Rossiter found most interesting was Julia. If eyes could speak, hers were rattling off words faster than Lady Jersey at a cozy tea for two. She pecked Harry on the cheek and whispered something in his ear.

Oglesby watched these goings-on with pinched lips and a disapproving frown. This was hardly the fashion in which one would wish to see one's betrothed carry on with another man.

"They have been friends since the cradle," Amanda said to the rector. "You mustn't mind Julia's *sisterly* fondness for Harry. We think nothing of it. All of our girls love him—as a brother."

As he watched the group around Major Druce, Oglesby seemed to manifest displeasure at his intended's behaviour. His neck stretched to its limit and his chin jutted out as far as it would go. He swallowed several times in quick succession, causing his Adam's apple to bob crazily.

"Quite an affectionate lady, that Miss Witton," Rossiter observed, standing at the rector's side. "You are to be felicitated, sir, on your choice of wife. I congratulate you on your good fortune."

Craning his head around to better view the tall lord, Oglesby pinned a simpering smile on his lips. "I fall to my knees every night and give thanks for my treasured bride." He slowly turned his head in Julia's direction. "The wedding won't be too soon for me." He moistened his lips, missing the hard look Rossiter gave him.

Amanda called her daughters to order, and introduced Harry to the other gentlemen. She began pairing off the young ladies with their escorts to dinner. Julia, of course, went with Oglesby. The bishop offered his arm to Faith. Harry had the good fortune to be allotted the two youngest Witton girls. He offered his arm to Marion, and Sarah fell in step at his side. Taking Lord Rossiter's arm again, Amanda led the way to the large dining room.

An extra setting had been laid for Harry by the very efficient Cleeves. Amanda directed everyone to their places with gracious waves this way and that.

After the general settling in had ceased, Julia found herself between Rossiter and Oglesby. The first course began.

"Dear Mother Witton," the rector commenced, "I was surprised that your eminent husband, the bishop, did not attend the grand fête at Carlton House. My uncle, the bishop of Durham, was honoured with an invitation." He dipped his spoon in the turtle soup and slurped greedily.

Grimacing a bit, Amanda said, "The bishop rendered his heartfelt regrets to the Regent, but with the wedding and Julia's, ah, sudden illness he could not possibly attend. Already word is trickling down from Town about the magnificent supper that was served." She winced when she heard the rector's all-too-audible consumption of his soup. "I do hope that you are enjoying your meal, Mr. Oglesby."

He sucked up some wine before replying. "I offer you my compliments, Mother Witton. Your cook is much better than mine. Mine is an idiot. She scarcely knows how to boil a turnip."

"A pity." Amanda looked at Oglesby's empty bowl and motioned for more to be served. "Have you thought of hiring another woman, a better cook?" She looked politely at him.

"I have, but these cooks get above themselves, quite uppity about the wage they will consent to work for. I refuse to pay above twenty pounds, four shillings a year for a woman to burn my bacon." He patted his betrothed on the back, as she seemed to be choking on her soup.

Amanda's smile became strained. "I have heard that the King is feeling much more the thing these days. One must feel a great amount of sorrow for him, though. Such a pity he has had to suffer that dreadful malady."

"Insanity *is* a dreadful malady, Mother Witton." Oglesby's tone sounded as if he had just climbed to his pulpit. "I have been told, by men who should know, that the Prince Regent might have caught that same malady from the King. The Regent's madness for spending money can only be attributed to a lapse in judgment. I've heard it said that insanity is highly contagious.''

Amanda appeared not to know how to take Mr. Oglesby's statement, but her eldest daughter had no such trouble.

"Are you suggesting that we are in danger of becoming insane? Nonsense, Mr. Oglesby. Pure nonsense.'' A mischievous smile began to light Julia's face, but she suppressed it. "I would have you know that Mama's aunt was held to be not quite right in her mind. But so far none of us has succumbed to spells of fancy, or walking about barefoot in the grass.''

"Barefoot, hey?'' Rossiter murmured in Julia's ear, as he looked down at some point beneath the table.

"The lord watches over his own, my dear Miss Witton,'' Oglesby stated. "But what is this about insanity in your family, Mother Witton?''

"My aunt was a mere eccentric, I assure you, sir.'' Amanda took a deep swallow of wine and looked helplessly down the board to the bishop. She knew that good manners prevented him from coming to her aid. It would never do to shout down the length of the table, as the rector was doing.

With the hint of insanity in the air, Oglesby commenced to quiz Amanda quite thoroughly upon the antecedents of the Witton family. If the family was prone to eccentrics and odd persons, then he wanted to know about them before the wedding.

Amanda began to clear the air of any suspicions, all the while aware that his lordship might be listening with the same avid attention as Mr. Oglesby.

Rossiter's attention, however, was elsewhere. He leaned toward Julia. "It seems that the worthy Mr. Oglesby hasn't a chivalrous nature," he observed quietly. "'Twould be a pity if he withdrew his suit merely at a hint of lunacy. That was not very wise of you. Mentioning your mother's aunt was a mistake."

"Oh?" Her eyes widened innocently.

He held up his quizzing-glass. "My dear Julia, you are a first-rate schemer. But one must ask, why do you wish to be rid of the worthy Oglesby now, after your long engagement?"

This question caused her to glance to the side at her betrothed, who was still entirely absorbed by what her mother was saying. She turned to Rossiter. "Have you a grudge against me, sir?" she hissed.

He shook his head.

"Then why in heaven are you so intent that I be shackled to the rector?"

The brow over the patch rose. "I was remiss in my thinking. I mistakenly thought that a bride these days has some say in who it is she marries. You must pardon my rash conclusions."

"Do you recall Lord Nelson's message to his men at Trafalgar?" Julia asked abruptly.

"'England expects every man will do his duty,'" he quoted softly.

She looked at his scar, momentarily diverted from her thoughts. Then she turned to gaze down the table to her father. "Do you suppose duty is any less important to England's womenfolk?" she said, when she assured herself that no one was yet listening to their words.

Thomas watched her face. "I daresay that duty is an even heavier weight upon the women than the men." He placed his hand on her arm and leaned nearer. "Remember that I stand your friend. Friends help each other out of the briars.''

The close scrutiny to which she subjected him would have undone a lesser man. But Thomas was made of a stronger fibre, the sort that could withstand attacks of knives, sabres—and the thorough stares of a bishop's daughter.

''I wonder,'' she murmured, lowering her gaze. She remained silent for the rest of the meal. Had she been more aware of her surroundings she would have noticed the questioning looks Harry was casting her. And she would have been acutely conscious of the approval which Oglesby bestowed upon her for her ladylike reserve.

At the completion of dinner, Amanda led her daughters to the main drawing-room. She soon had Faith before the harp and Marion warming up her vocal cords with a few light tunes. As usual, Sarah retired early to her room and, as usual, she had some beneficial reading to do.

Julia found herself at her mother's side for a tête-á-tête.

''Now, dearest, I needn't tell you how upsetting it was for Mr. Oglesby to hear that your great-aunt was a bit...peculiar. After much persuasion, I explained everything to his satisfaction.'' Amanda dabbed her upper lip as she remembered the ordeal. One must sacrifice for one's children, she reasoned.

''I promise not to say the word insanity to Mr. Oglesby,'' Julia said solemnly.

''I knew you would do just as you ought. Now...oh dear, how shall I begin?'' Amanda's hands fluttered helplessly. She clasped them together and cleared her throat. ''I want you to let Mr. Oglesby kiss you.'' She sat back, greatly relieved to have the worst over. ''This is a liberty I would not normally allow my daughters, but you *are* betrothed.'' Her voice trailed away, as if that reasoning explained it all. ''You see, Julia, when Mr. Oglesby saw you kiss Harry he was quite distraught. One shouldn't kiss another man in the presence of one's intended. It is not at all the thing. Will you do that little favour for me?"

Julia swallowed hard. Would that she could do that favour for her without doing it for him, Julia said to herself. Aloud she said, "I shall try my best."

"I know you will and I do not ask for anything more." Amanda cleared her throat. "It is a lovely night for a stroll. You have my permission to show Mr. Oglesby the garden."

A twinkle appeared in Julia's eyes. "Mama, how do you suggest I go about getting Mr. Oglesby to kiss me?"

"Well—" Amanda caught herself before she took the bait completely. She glared at her daughter. "If you give me some taradiddle about knowing nothing of kissing, I'll box your ears. You read novels. Now, no more of your jokes. This is a serious matter."

"A very serious matter, Mama."

There was an air of gravity about Julia that seemed to satisfy Amanda. "I am pleased that you look upon this delicate business in such a light. Since Mr. Oglesby is here, it is your duty to extend whatever courtesies are necessary for his comfort and enjoyment. Some mention was made during dinner of an excursion to Glastonbury Tor."

"Oh?"

Amanda looked at Julia queerly. "Yes, a great deal of mention was made. Weren't you attending? You must pay more heed to Mr. Oglesby. I am sure he would be pleased to see the Tor. Taking care of his desires should be foremost in your mind."

"Yes, Mama."

"One more thing, my dear. No more kissing Harry, even on the cheek. I absolutely forbid it."

"Yes, Mama." Julia's tone was a touch too meek, but her smile conveyed reassurance.

Their chat ended satisfactorily. Julia's acquiescence settled the matter nicely.

Amanda went about directing her daughters in the various occupations she wished to see them engaged in when the gentlemen rejoined them. Faith was to play the harp, Marion was to play a game of noddy with Lord Rossiter, and Julia was to hold a piece of needlework, yet not set one stitch. For Amanda wished to achieve a pleasing look, not finish a sampler.

"Mama," Marion called from her place next to Faith by the harp, "this artful posing is silly. I had not thought you the sort to attempt these obvious matchmaking ploys. Yet, this . . ." With a sweeping motion, she indicated the contrived tableau.

The good lady of the house stiffened at the aspersions cast upon her good intentions. "My dears," Amanda said, viewing her daughters, "Marion is quite right. You have the look of stuffed game." She waved her hand dismissively. "Do whatever pleases you. But I would remind you of your duties to our guests when they join us." She sent a pointed look to Julia, who smiled and gazed down at the needle in her hand.

A short time later, the bishop led the gentlemen into the drawing-room. Oglesby was close by the bishop's shoulder and it appeared that his one desire was to stay there. Trailing behind the two men of the Church came Rossiter and Harry in quiet conversation. They seemed to be on good terms with each other.

Following their mother's instructions, Marion coaxed Harry into singing a duet without too much resistance, and Rossiter offered to turn the pages for Faith as she accompanied them on the pianoforte.

In a manoeuvre to rival any general in the field, the bishop detached the rector from his side and sent him off to Julia at the far end of the room. Naturally Oglesby chose to sit close to her on the sofa where her mama had left her. Unfortunately the discarded needle from the cast-aside sampler found its way into the rector's posterior. The assembled company was treated to a jig as Oglesby jumped about.

"Oh dear!" Julia put a hand to her cheek. "How careless of me. Poor Mr. Oglesby, are you injured, sir?"

He leaned on the sofa at an odd angle and plucked out a small needle with a length of blue thread through its eye. "No! No, it is a mere flesh wound."

"My dear bishop," Amanda exclaimed, "we must send for the physician. Mr. Oglesby's wound must be looked at." She wrung her hands.

"It is quite unnecessary." Oglesby waved Amanda's suggestion aside as he eyed the shiny, new needle from the safe distance of his extended arm. He placed the offending object in Julia's hand. "I pray that in the future you will take care where you leave your needlework."

She smiled innocently at the rector and put away her stitchery. "You are such a patient man, sir. I hope that you will show this same forebearance when I make some little mistake after we are wed. Often the strangest things happen to me."

"What sort of things?" he asked, eyeing her suspiciously.

She bit her lip and looked helpless. "Oh dear! Nothing to signify, just little mishaps. But they aren't my fault. It is ridiculous to think that I had anything to do with Farmer John's cow going dry. You don't think I'm, ah, different, do you, kind Mr. Oglesby?" She looked at him with wide eyes.

"A cow went dry?" He gazed at her dubiously.

"Yes, is that not silly? All this talk in the parish about mystic powers is nonsense. Utter nonsense!" She leaned a bit closer to him. "I do look forward to our Midsummer Eve merrymaking. I chose the festival as a fitting time to celebrate our nuptials."

"I do not approve of this Midsummer masque and festivities."

"Oh, that is a pity. The bishop so delights in the innocent revelry. He will be sorely disappointed."

Oglesby bit his lip. "If that is the way of it, then I shall not object to observing the festival—in a reserved manner, as is my custom."

"There, you see? You are a tolerant man." She patted his arm. "How could anything bad happen with such a man as you nearby to lean on? You can provide the kindness I need." Julia made a curious crossing design in the air with her hands, then sat back with a satisfied sigh.

"What did you just do with your hands?"

"Do? Nothing, I assure you." She smiled at him. "Would you approve of seeing our garden, sir? I daresay a turn on the terrace would be beneficial for your injury." Julia rose with a sweep of clinging satin. She found the rector at her side urging her toward the long windows.

As the couple disappeared behind the draperies, Faith fumbled at the keyboard, striking a jarring chord. Her eyes, as well as those of the others in the room, watched the curtain drop into place. Her gaze was drawn to Marion, who shrugged.

"I find it warm tonight," Faith said, grasping the courage to speak in a carrying voice. "Would you be so kind, Lord Rossiter, as to let in some cooling air?"

He bowed to Faith's request and strolled over to the windows. Moving to the place where the rector had led Julia out, he drew back the drapes and eased open the casement.

The duet at the pianoforte continued in a half-hearted fashion. Rossiter seemed content to hear the music from a distance. The murmur of voices from outside came floating to him.

"How captivating is the night," Julia said, leaning out over the rail toward the silver rays of moonlight. "I find there is an odd quality about the moon that makes me a touch irrational. Have you ever heard the word lycanthropy, Mr. Oglesby?"

He looked at her in a puzzled manner. "No."

"You haven't?" She sighed with relief. "I do not want you to listen to any of the talk. Promise? I cannot help the way I am. It is the moon. I do the strangest things when the moon is full."

Oglesby caught hold of Julia's hand. "My dear, dear Miss Witton, something strange happens to me when I am near you."

"Is that so? I would wager that it is the moon's effect upon you." She moved away from him. "I go quite mad myself by it. Why, once I had the impulse to bay at the full moon. Was not that the strangest thing?"

His eyes widened at the words. "Do you always get these wild impulses?"

"Wild impulses? I?" Julia placed her hand artfully to her bosom and moved closer to Oglesby. "Has someone been talking to you about me already?"

He drew back. "What do you mean?"

"Nothing, truly." She smiled in a beguiling fashion, then ran to the steps leading down to the garden. She stood poised on the top step. "Merciful heavens! I want to throw out my arms and submit to wild abandonment." She threw her arms wide and ran back to the rector. Turning and spinning about Oglesby, Julia moved with unknowing allure.

As she passed before him he reached out and caught her to his shallow chest. "Julia, my one desire, I must have you!" With surprising force the rector embraced her.

"You... you want me?" she asked in a startled voice.

"Yes! Yes!" Oglesby tried to kiss her.

She jerked her head away to avoid his searching mouth.

"Mr. Oglesby! Stop, I command you! You go too far."

Frustrated by her movements, his roving eyes caught sight of richer treasure. Relentlessly his lips moved over her neck and down toward his goal.

She wrenched out of his grasp. Then with all her might, she struck the rector full in the face.

Oglesby sprang back with a yelp of pain from the force of her blow. Drops of blood began to trickle down to his upper lip. "By all that's holy, look what you've done!"

"Do not talk to me of piety, you wicked, wicked man."

"How dare you!"

"How dare *you*!" She looked ready to come at him again.

He backed away from her. Into the drawing room he stepped, holding a handkerchief to his nose. The bit of fabric showed signs of vivid colour as each drop of blood stained it. Muffled sounds of excited anger came from beneath the wad of linen as Mr. Oglesby marched, with his stiff neck tilted back, across the room and out the double doors into the hall.

"Emory," Amanda exclaimed, jumping up from beside the bishop, "the man is seriously hurt!" She hurried after the rector, calling for Cleeves as she went.

In the ensuing commotion, Rossiter slipped out through the long window. He found Julia straightening her gown.

"Was I mistaken? Did I hear a slap?"

The muscles in her cheeks danced a little. "Why, I dare-say you did. I was being annoyed by a pest and had to swat it away."

His lips strained against each other as he struggled for control. "Is that the wisest way to pique a man's inter-est?"

Julia smoothed back her hair. "I do not always choose the wisest course. But one does try to learn from past ex-periences. I advise you to keep your distance, Rossiter."

"Do not say that you place me in the same class as our worthy, but amorous, rector?"

"Oh, no. You are unique, milord. Besides, you know how to kiss." She smiled. "Fascinating!" She held up her hand when he began to move closer. "But in my present state I would receive your advances in the same manner as I did Mr. Oglesby's."

"The man is your betrothed."

"So he is." She looked at him, yet gave none of her thoughts away by so much as a flicker of an eyelid.

It was his turn to regard her silently. After what seemed a long time, he asked, "Would you walk with me?"

Quietly she took his arm and together they wandered the various paths of the garden. They did not speak. The un-derstanding they reached came without words.

With reluctance, she drew a little away from him. "You are good company, Lord Rossiter."

"Thomas, remember?"

She nodded, but would not look at him. "I remember." She peeked up with a wavering smile. "I doubt that I shall ever forget you . . . Thomas." She shook herself, as if to re-call a task not yet completed. "It grows late. My mother will be wondering what has become of us. Perhaps you should go in first. I shall just wait out here for a little." She walked away from him, moving toward the summer-house.

Then she turned back to him. "What o'clock is it, milord?"

He looked at her curiously as he pulled out his timepiece. "It is near ten, miss. Why?"

"Why? Why, I should hate to keep you from your bed. All that studying must tire you."

"I am never too tired for bed." One corner of his mouth lifted into a half-smile.

She looked nonplussed. "Well, then you will want to return to all that *fascinating* research."

"I am content here."

Her glance was impatient. "I wish to be alone."

"Blister me, have you arranged a tryst with the worthy Oglesby?"

"Don't be absurd! I merely desire a few moments of quiet reflection before retiring." Julia's expression became desperate. "Would you go away. Please!" She turned and made her way to the summer-house. At the sound of his step behind her, she stopped and confronted him. "Lord Rossiter, Thomas, I desire that you leave me."

"What sort of gentleman would I be if I abandoned you here in this lonely spot at this time of the night?" He shook his head, appearing quite serious about carrying out his duties as escort. "No, Julia, my conscience forbids such shabby treatment." He grinned at her. "We one-eyed demons have a strange sense of what is proper."

"'Tis strange indeed! What could possibly happen to me out here?"

He looked to the heavens, as if seeking a kindred understanding. "She tempts Fate too far. What could happen, she asks." He looked down at her from his celestial communication and flashed a wicked smile. Ever so slowly, he moved closer.

"Thomas, stop this nonsense." She nearly stamped her foot. "You cannot go about taking liberties with me whenever we are alone."

His arm encircled her waist. "'Tis the moon. When it's full I am driven to madness." He pulled her to him.

"How dare—"

His mouth covered hers. She would have striven to make a strong protest, but his lips felt so deliciously good moving over hers that she quite lost her senses.

"Why do you keep doing that?" she asked, when at last he gave her a chance to catch her breath.

"It is becoming a habit I am loath to break."

From the garden, the crunch of gravel beneath someone's feet caught their attention. The bright red of a regimental coat flitted briefly into sight before disappearing into the darkness. Rossiter smiled at Harry's retreating back.

Julia watched Harry leave with a sinking heart. Would she never have a chance to speak to him alone? She looked at Thomas's satisfied expression and wondered if he knew about her rendezvous with Harry.

"Shall we go in?" he asked politely, as if nothing untoward had passed.

CHAPTER TEN

"I QUITE FORGIVE YOU, dear Miss Witton," Mr. Oglesby said, as he wobbled by her side. The rector's gait was quite odd, as he seldom rode. Staying astride his horse until they reached Glastonbury Tor had been a difficult exercise for him.

He took Julia by the arm and led her away from the others of the party, who were gathering at the Chalice Well after dismounting or climbing down from the carriage. "Last night's foray was a result of your little malady caused by the moon," he whispered. "I advise you to stay indoors during the evening hours. It's not healthy for a lady to cavort about in the moonlight." He pursed his lips. "This scheme of a Midsummer masque is an ill-advised venture for someone of your disposition. I have given it much thought. Your mother is a woman of unusual good sense."

"How kind of you to say so."

"Your father, the bishop, made an excellent choice in her. But this festival until dawn is unseemly. I cannot approve of it."

Julia's hand clenched in the folds of her riding habit. "Yet the bishop has given his approval. I do not understand all the fuss you make, Mr. Oglesby."

"Fuss? I make no fuss. Why, I revere the bishop's judgment in all things. You must tell him so."

"I daresay he would be pleased to hear that praise from your own lips."

"Do you think so?"

"Indeed I do!"

Oglesby stretched his neck importantly. "I pride myself on my ability to get on well with my fellows in the Church. One must make his own way in this world. If my geniality with my superiors in the clergy reaps the benefits of an elevation of rank, then I shall thank Providence for that trait, for one must view such a gift as a godsend. Not every man can ingratiate himself in the manner that I do."

"Yes, I remember my father saying some of those same words only this morning."

"Did he? Excellent!" He took her hand and attempted to kiss it. But his lips fell upon his empty palm as she drew away from him. "You mustn't be shy with me, as you were last night. You are my greatest asset. With you at my side I can look to the highest heights. Believe me, dear Miss Witton, a man who marries advantageously can achieve anything in this world." He looked around to be sure no one was watching them, then tried stealing a kiss.

"For shame, Mr. Oglesby! You forget yourself."

A licentious grin flashed across his thin face. "This modesty of yours is quite charming, but quite foolish." He inspected her body from head to toe, pausing over her tempting curves along the way. "In a short time you will be mine to command as I will. I do so look forward to the day that we will be one, in spirit—and in flesh."

Julia watched him run his tongue over his lips. The action and words made her shudder.

"Are you well, dear Miss Witton? Should we perhaps wait in your mother's carriage while the others continue with this ridiculous excursion? We could pass the time quite pleasantly." He leered. "After all, one should not emerge from the sickroom too soon after an illness. You must be fit for the wedding . . . and all."

For a moment she looked at him. Thoughts of laying claim to a relapse came to her. A protracted illness would put the wedding off, but would it put Mr. Oglesby off? Maybe if she had to travel to some warm climate for a cure, then he might lose patience and look elsewhere. Yet somehow she doubted that happy outcome. Once a man like Oglesby had fallen upon such a favourable situation, he was not likely to move on.

"I shall do well enough," she said. "The climb to the top is just what I need." The others, including Bounder, had already begun the steep ascent. Yet Julia paused for a moment at the Chalice Well, gazing into its depths. Her betrothed stood by her side. "Do you know what the locals call this place?" she asked, in an awed tone. "The Blood Spring."

Stepping back from the well, Oglesby looked ready to bolt up the hill, away from the mystical spot. "Now, my dear Miss Witton, compose yourself."

"I have seen many marvels occur because of this water. 'Tis said it has venerable powers for healing. Did you know it is believed the Holy Grail is buried at the bottom?"

"I make it my practice not to believe in that sort of folderol." He looked along the path that led up the hill, as the others moved farther away from them. "Let us go now. We must catch up with your saintly mother." He pulled Julia away from the well.

As they walked along, Julia kept a safe distance from the rector. She set a brisk pace, making the going difficult for him.

Oglesby repeatedly tried to catch her hand. Frustrated in his efforts, he began to prose. "When we are wed, I shall turn your mind to more fitting topics of consideration. I find you far too concerned with wonder-workings and enchantments." He stopped to catch his breath. "I shall form new thoughts in your mind. I pride myself on a knowledge above the ordinary. It shall be my pleasure to impart a portion of my learning for your benefit. Though I do not hold with these modern theories of educating females above the gentle accomplishments, I shall not object to instructing you in matters of greater import."

"My father allows me to read the *Times*," Julia stated, a veiled challenge in her voice.

The rector's eyes nearly shot from their sockets. "Good lord! He does?"

"Father abhors ignorant females. He subscribes to the theory that females should be enlightened. Why, even Sarah is quite well read. She reads book upon book under specific instruction from Father." She smiled in a pleasant way.

Pursing his lips together, Oglesby tucked his chin down, deep in thought. "I shall have to give this matter grave consideration."

Julia walked ahead of him with a jaunty step.

A short time later they reached the rest of the group, who were halfway up the Tor waiting for the couple. Sarah held Bounder's leash, as the mastiff sniffed about the ground. Sitting on a large rock, Amanda looked ready to continue. But the shallow-chested rector was huffing and puffing.

"Mother Witton," Oglesby gasped, mopping his brow, "I see this climb is too taxing—" he drew a deep breath and continued "—too taxing for one with your delicate nature. We must abandon this ill-conceived expedition, if only to spare you the rigours of the ascent." A droplet of sweat ran down his nose.

Amanda stood up. "My daughters and I are country ladies, sir, capable of walking great distances if need be. The bishop suggested we see the view from the top, and see the view we shall.'' She took Mr. Oglesby by the arm and helped him along the trail.

Stumbling to a halt after a few paces, Oglesby declared, "I do not believe I shall attempt to climb this odd mound." He turned to Julia. "You have not been well. I shall keep you company while the others go above. Pray excuse us, Mother Witton."

Sarah glowered at the rector. "How paltry!"

A general outcry followed her words. But the more the others objected, the more Oglesby became entrenched in his refusal to ascend the Tor or allow his bride that pleasure. Furthermore, he took advantage of the delay to edify the company with a discourse on the proper comportment of young ladies.

Drifting to the edge of the small congregation, Julia found herself at Lord Rossiter's side. The quizzical look upon his face was unsettling, but she retained her equanimity.

"One can only wonder at the nature of married life with the worthy Mr. Oglesby." Thomas looked down at her, his patch gleaming in the sunlight. "Are you ready to cry off—yet?"

Deliberately, she pretended to misunderstand him. "One does not postpone a wedding. It is bad luck."

He placed a hand in the middle of her back and moved her away from the general company. "It is also bad luck to marry an idiot. But I see you are bent on doing so."

"I have given my word—my pledge—that I will marry Oglesby. I am bound by honour to do my duty. Seneca believed, as do I, that a woman's honour is equally as great and energetic as a man's."

"Is it so? Most curious. I daresay that is how your mother got caught in this imbroglio." He shot her a dark look. "Blast it, you are not a horse-faced shrew to be let go to any man who'll take you. Have you considered heading for the border with the major?''

Julia shot him a startled glance. Did he know? she wondered. ''What a nonsensical notion. Harry would never agree to such a suggestion, even if I were bird-witted enough to ask.''

''Never?'' He looked closely at her. ''And you would have to do the asking? I thought you and the major were on better terms than that.'' He fixed his gaze upon her and shook his head sadly.

''It must annoy you, milord, not to know everything about everyone. Harry is the best of good fellows, but he would hardly fly to the border with me.''

''Yes, I thought him a man of good sense.''

As if aware that he was being discussed, Harry fell back to join them. ''You know, Julia, one would almost think that fellow Oglesby's a Roundhead. His notions of propriety verge on the puritan.'' He watched the rector strike his fist to the palm of his hand. ''He is like to drive the girls into taking up the ways of sin with all his platitudes.''

Julia directed her glare at Thomas instead of Harry. ''Recall that you are speaking of the man I am to marry.''

''That's another thing,'' Harry went on. ''What could your father have been thinking of when he consented to the match?''

''A touch of dyspepsia,'' suggested Thomas playfully.

''Undoubtedly,'' Harry agreed.

Julia glowered at the men. ''I daresay I should be flattered that you two view my engagement as a result of indigestion.''

''Well now,'' Harry said, ''even you must admit the rector leaves a bad taste in one's mouth.'' He grinned at her and added, ''So to speak. By the by, has he tried to kiss you yet?''

Thomas leaned toward Harry and said, "I detect a bit of annoyance in the eyes of this bishop's daughter. Beware, friend."

"By jove," Harry replied in a teasing voice, "I do believe you're in the right of it, Rossiter."

"And you call yourselves gentlemen—ha!" Julia stalked away from them and headed for her betrothed. "Mr. Oglesby, I *am* climbing the Tor. You may accompany me if you wish, sir. Come along, everyone," she called to the others. "Are you coming?" she asked the rector, her tone so brisk that it left him with his mouth agape. Turning to lead the way, Julia caught Thomas watching her. If he thought her a managing female, so be it.

Upon reaching the height of the mount that dominated the surrounding countryside, the group took a long pause to catch their breaths and rest. Oglesby looked completely done in. Even his stiff neck sagged forward in exhaustion.

Amanda, looking conscience-stricken, gave the rector aid in the form of her vinaigrette. The others began to roam about and take in the view. Sarah and Bounder headed for the tower on the summit—the last remnant of the church built to honour St. Michael.

"Your intended is unfit to accompany you, Miss Witton," Thomas observed after giving Oglesby a casual glance. "Shall we?" He offered his arm. When she placed her hand on it, he said, "I am glad to see you do not bear grudges."

Her expression became less chill as she looked about. Since the day was unimpaired by low-hanging clouds, the view from atop the Tor was magnificent. They could see for miles in all directions. The Quantock Hills, the Bristol Channel, some ten miles away, and the Mendip Hills were all visible in panoramic beauty.

"I rather feel as if the world has been laid at my feet," remarked Thomas.

"I love it up here." Julia shifted to look at him and smiled in her engaging way. The smile slackened a bit when she realized she wanted to share her pleasure with him.

"What are you thinking, Julia?"

"I was merely wondering about the oddities of life. You know, my lord, for all of your irksome ways, I count you my friend. Is that not curious?"

"You find it odd that you have a particular fondness for a maimed old soldier, hey?"

She laughed at his description of himself. "Are you trying to soften my heart again with this talk of your old injuries? I tell you, they matter little to me."

"What a pity. I was hoping to wring some compassion from you for heroic deeds done for King and country."

"I am of the opinion that you got your scar from a brawl in an unsavoury taproom while defending the name of some tainted flower of delight. The use of the cane I find intriguing." She looked at him intently. "You aren't still suffering any pain, are you?"

"Ah, the light of compassion at last. All is not lost. Shall we hie away, sweet damsel?" He motioned toward the distant hills with his cane. "Would you leave kith and kin, and the worthy Oglesby, for life with one some call a demon?"

She watched him, enjoyment dancing in her eyes. "Milord, would that I could, but I dare not. Even now the enemy is at our gates." She looked beyond his shoulder at the reclining Mr. Oglesby, who was being fanned by her mother.

"Shall we away, my lady, while there is still time?"

She shook her head and took on a sorrowful expression. "Nay, brave knight, for we must tarry a while longer. If you are one of Arthur's knights, then you shall remain steadfast and true to the end. But if you are not of the Round Table, then your courage will fail you and you shall be as the dust, blown this way and that." She walked a little away from him. "Did you know that Harry, Lucian and I used to come here to play, making believe that we, too, were knights of yore? It is believed that King Arthur came here to die. There are many tales of bravery in these parts."

"But none so touching," he said, coming up behind her, "as the tale of the bishop's daughter who would give herself, out of duty, to the spindle-shanked clergyman."

"Thomas, there is something in me that makes me want to take my own way in things. I obey my parents, after my own fashion, but they do not rule me. Though I had never met the rector, I did agree to this betrothal. If it ends, that too shall be upon my head."

"You wish me to retire from the field and allow you to take your own course?"

"I knew you would understand." She searched his face. "I've a feeling that I can call on you when I need help, and you'll be there, ready to ride your charger full tilt and rescue this headstrong maiden from her folly."

He made a courtly bow. "It shall be as the lady wishes."

At that moment she wished Oglesby to the devil, but she would bide her time, though the day of the wedding came ever closer. She wondered if her ability to roust her betrothed would be any match for his tenacious desire to retain his position, for nothing seemed to deter him. She became even more determined to succeed. With this in mind, she went to her mother to offer her aid in tending the rector.

By a means not quite known to the unfortunate man, he was rendered more uncomfortable by her tender ministrations. When she offered to loosen his neckcloth, he found himself choking from its tightness after she finished. Then she somehow managed to tread on his hand, then tear his second-best coat.

"You are not well, Mr. Oglesby," Julia said. "You mustn't tax yourself before the wedding...and all. Pray allow his lordship to help you down to the carriage." As she made to help him up, Julia let the rector fall and land on his back. "How dreadful. Here, let me help you."

Oglesby scrambled away from her. "No! For pity's sake, stay away from me. I want none of your hoaxing and tricks!"

Thrusting her vinaigrette under his nose, Amanda said, "'Tis the sun. He has had too much of it and is out of his head with fever."

Before descending, Julia called to Harry, letting him know of their intentions. He waved them on and turned to his two lovely companions, Faith and Marion. Sarah and Bounder, meanwhile, were not in sight. They apparently were still exploring the ruins of St. Michael's. Scanning the ground, Sarah wandered about the ruins, hopeful of finding a token of ages past. After a time she let Bounder loose from his leash, and he frisked off on his own business. Alone, she entered the tower through the doorless portal. Within the cold stone walls of the tower a chilling instinct prompted her to turn around, but as she did so a stranger confronted her. She puckered her lips to whistle for Bounder, but the sound that emerged was but a mere rasp of air. The thin, ferret-faced man approaching her looked disreputable.

"How did you get up here?" she asked boldly. "I did not see you come up the main path."

"That's as it should be," the man replied. "Tell me, missie, you bein' from the manor house of the bishop so you'd know, have you heard talk of a pouch, fancy and leather? I lost it a few night past. Been in my family for years. Lost the thing around the manor house, I did. You wouldn't be knowing its whereabouts, now would you, missie?''

"What is your name?"

He frowned and rubbed the tip of his nose, as if debating. "I go by the name of Bateman."

"You say you lost a pouch, Mr. Bateman."

"Aye, with some letters in it from me dear ol' mum. You seen it?''

"No. Now, go away, or I shall call my friend, the major, who is a hero of the War."

"That armless cripple? You listen to me, missie, I needs that pouch back. If you find it I'll give you a handsome reward, coin of the Realm."

"If I found anything I would give it to my father, who would then hand it over to the magistrate."

The man stepped closer to Sarah, baring his yellow teeth. "See here, if I don't have that pouch soon, something right awful will be befallin' your dog. A pity if he took sick and died." The man gave Sarah a sly look. "I've watched you. You're clever as a cat—hugger-mugger to a tittle. You see things. Find me that pouch. Understand?''

Sarah nodded and edged around him.

"Good. Now, if you go and cry bacon to the bishop, that major, or anybody else like 'em, I'll have your hide *and* your dog's. I'll be visitin' you again. See you got something to tell me, else—'' He drew his fingers across his throat.

Before Sarah quite realized it, the man faded into the shadows of the walls and disappeared from sight. She shivered at the ominous threat left hanging in the air. Slowly she backed out of the tower.

"Bounder!" she called shrilly. "Here, boy! Come here!" The mastiff raced toward her from the terraced grounds below. Before he could reach her side she ran to the path leading down. "Come everyone," Sarah yelled to Harry and her two sisters. "Hurry! I think a storm is coming."

Marion looked about, then turned a puzzled face to Harry. "Do you see any clouds? I wonder what has taken hold of the girl? Why, she looks as if the devil were after her."

"Maybe she saw the ghost of the headless monk." Harry's voice had an eerie quality, and Marion and Faith chided him for his teasing as he escorted them down.

At the foot of the Tor, the party reassembled. Oglesby had collapsed in Mrs. Witton's carriage, and lay there moaning and complaining. Julia went to see how he fared.

"Are you feeling more the thing, sir?" she asked, as she placed her hands on the door of the barouche. "Was it not kind of Lord Rossiter to help you down?"

"Don't talk to me of that man. He is an insufferable bore. Has no notion of how to treat one who is ill any more than you do." Petulantly he threw an arm over his eyes. "But what can one expect—the man is a veritable Tulip. I doubt his thoughts go beyond the fall of his cravat."

"I see that you want to be alone. I am upsetting you with my chatter. Until later, then." Julia left him and sought out Harry.

After detaching him from Marion's and Faith's company, she said, "I should not be speaking to you, Harry Druce." She glared at him. "To keep a lady waiting once until the small hours before dawn was reprehensible enough, but to repeat it is unpardonable."

"I went to the summer-house last night. But—now, I may be mistaken—you appeared to be occupied with Lord Rossiter. Yes, I believe we can call such doings an occupation, for I saw no sign of your trying to give it up. Is that the way the wind blows?"

"Enough! If you wish to know which way the wind blows, consult a weather vane. I'll have you know, Harry, that after everyone had gone to bed, I went to the summerhouse and waited and waited for you. Where were you?"

"I was with Lord Rossiter."

"What!"

Harry grinned. "Rossiter was a busy fellow last night. After wooing you, he waylaid me. We broke a bottle and played cards for hours."

"Men! How you can drink all night, then ride the next day is beyond me."

"Oh, Rossiter doesn't imbibe deeply. But, you see how it was. I couldn't leave."

Julia nodded and sighed. "We still have to talk." She moved to her mount as the groom brought it up to her, and stroked the mare's nose.

"I've a few words for you, too," Harry retorted.

"Ah, Major Druce," Rossiter said, coming up behind them. "Miss Marion needs some assistance. I swear I am all thumbs today. Would you be so kind?"

Harry looked from Julia to Lord Rossiter and smiled. He set his hat at a rakish angle and went over to Marion.

"Fine-looking fellow, the major," Rossiter observed. "Even without the arm, he seems to do very well for himself."

"Major Druce is a very capable man in all situations. We have ceased to even notice the reminder he carries of the War." She looked thoughtful. "It bothers him more than us."

"A man's pride is not easily reasoned away."

She gazed at Thomas in a speculating manner. "I wonder where the chink is in your armour, my lord?"

He held his hand over his heart. "It is here. Would you care to try to pierce it, Miss Witton?"

She stepped away from him, flustered. "I am certain that if I tried I would discover that it was made of cold, hard stone. You are a heartless wretch, with more tears shed over you, so I have been told, than any man has the right to expect. I am a fool to pay heed to any of your words." She made ready to mount her mare.

"Aye, there's no accounting for taste, is there?" He glanced in Oglesby's direction. Then, instead of offering a gloved hand to help her up, Thomas placed his hands around her waist and lifted her onto the saddle. "Not as light as I thought you'd be."

Her cheeks flamed with colour. With a little awkwardness, she threw her leg over the pommel and smoothed the full skirt of her riding habit, all the while aware of Rossiter's regard.

A smile played over his lips. "I doubt the worthy Mr. Oglesby will be able to carry you over the threshold. Perhaps I should appoint myself as his deputy."

"You would not dare," she whispered.

The patch flashed wickedly. Thomas looked at her in a speculating fashion. "Have you not yet learned that I would dare anything?" He smiled at her again, before turning to his mount.

IT WAS A SHORT WHILE LATER that the ferret-faced man, Bateman, returned to the abandoned inn near Wookey Hole. He reported his afternoon's work to Philippe Vodrey.

"*Mon dieu*! You worthless rodent!" Philippe played with the pistol on the table before him. But in the end he fought his impulse. He would need the lout until this affair was finished. "I want you to stay away from that child of the bishop's. I do not wish to rouse Rossiter to action. He thinks he is clever, but I shall teach him who is the cleverer." He looked at Bateman with disdain. "Even with a pair of fools as my henchmen, I shall win the day and be the first to have the pouch."

"Philippe!" Trixie slammed the door against the wall as she thrust her way into the taproom. "Philippe, there is a rat in my room. Do you hear me? A rat!"

"The whole of the country can hear you," he said, a fixed smile on his lips. "My beauty, do not fret. Stokes will kill the rat. You must have patience, my sweet." He took her hand to dutifully kiss it.

She pulled away and glared at him. "I am done with patience, with suffering for love. I am used to a very different sort of life. I was not meant to live in a hovel. If you do not know how to see to my needs, then I can always return to Fitz. My husband may be a bore, but he would never treat me so roughly."

"Just a little longer, my pet. Soon all of France will worship you, the pure goddess of beauty. Poets will extol your grace and virtue. Artists will clamour to capture your perfect features. Just wait a little."

She pouted. "Oh, very well. But you must promise to stop locking my door at night. It frightens me."

"But, my cherished one, I must save you from these louts. Trust me to do what is best."

Trixie tossed her head and flounced out of the room.

Philippe sipped a glass of wine thoughtfully. He quickly forgot about Trixie. His mind was wrestling with matters of greater importance. Bateman had been wrong about the bishop's youngest daughter. She knew nothing.

But the eldest one bore watching. She was up to something out of the ordinary. Had she not waited last night at the summer-house for someone who never came? And, most significantly, Rossiter gave the lady special notice. If the fop was interested in her, then so was Philippe. There was talk in the neighbourhood of a masked ball, a Midsummer festival. Philippe's expression became more cunning and more menacing as he began to plan.

CHAPTER ELEVEN

FILTERING THROUGH THE TREES that lined Lovers' Walk, the setting sun's mellow rays played over the meadow beyond the manor house. On the freshly scythed grass stood the bishop and his wife, surveying the preparations for the Midsummer Eve festivities.

"Amanda, my dear," the bishop said, "you have outdone yourself this time. I particularly like the garlands of wildflowers."

A smile teased at her lips. "This year's gala will be better than the last." She watched a line of servants place platters of food on the roughly constructed tables of planks and sawhorses.

The bishop took his wife around to the colourful canvas booths that encircled the open field. Each booth offered a different amusement for the guests to indulge in, such as having the initials of one's true love revealed by dropping molten lead into cold water.

"I do not think that Mr. Oglesby approves of our celebration of this festival of St. John," the bishop observed.

"He is not used to our ways in the west country. I am sure that it is his...very firm sense of right that makes him seem condemning."

"He certainly has his own views on a great many subjects. I find him overeager to enlighten me about them all."

"Oh, dear, has he been plaguing you? How vexing!" Amanda cast her husband an anxious look.

He patted her hand. "Come, let us see if Cleeves has achieved a higher wood pile than last year's."

They moved to the centre of the meadow where a large heap of wood had been amassed for the midnight bonfire. The top of it reached beyond the bishop's head.

Approaching softly, Cleeves came to stand behind the bishop. He coughed gently. "Is everything satisfactory, my lord?"

"Quite, Cleeves. You have followed my good lady's wishes with your usual thoroughness." The bishop looked down at his own garb—that of a shepherd, complete with staff. "If only Julia hadn't insisted we all come in costume, I might enjoy this night without a qualm."

Amanda straightened the bishop's smock. "Now, my dear sir, you promised to wear whatever I chose to put on you."

He took Amanda by the hand and surveyed her costume. "My one solace is that I shall go unnoticed with you by my side, dear lady." Indeed, she had found the perfect gown to wear as his shepherdess, a rather elaborate mass of satin that no shepherdess would have dreamed of soiling by tending sheep.

With his neck stretched to its usual height, Oglesby made his way over the grass toward them with his stiff-legged step. He had humoured Mother Witton's wishes by fastening a black mask over his censorious eyes. But to pacify his soul he chose to wear his black coat and breeches. Around his neck was tied a black cravat, a clear indication of his mournful attitude toward the heathenish affair.

"Mr. Oglesby, have you received sad tidings?" Amanda asked, concern shadowing her eyes. "Have you learned of the passing of a close family member? If so, then we shall all have to go into black gloves. Not that I would not do so quite willingly, but the wedding..." All the preparations that had been made flashed through her head. She dreaded the chore of cancelling them all, so near the date of the nuptials.

"I am not mourning a loss in my family, ma'am." Oglesby touched his cravat. "I have chosen to wear what I deemed the proper attire for this night's revelry."

Cleeves's eyes widened. He withdrew with haste.

The bishop leaned on his staff to gaze more closely at the cleric before him. "This night's revelry is also held in honour of your approaching marriage to my daughter. One would surmise by your dress, sir, that you are mourning that event."

"My lord bishop," the rector whimpered, "that was not my intent. Sir, you must believe that I look forward with the greatest anticipation to the joining of our two families. Why, in little more than a sennight I shall take your lovely daughter and make her mine. I count the days."

"As do I." Amanda began to cipher the exact number.

Oglesby sighed. "I long for the joining." He gasped, startled by his own words and the image they evoked. Pray to heaven that the bishop did not take offence. "What I mean to say is that I am so eager to take Miss Witton—" At the raised eyebrows of his future in-laws he sputtered and quickly added, "—that is, take Miss Witton as my wife. The days do not go by fast enough."

Amanda blushed delicately. "One must go slowly with a new bride, sir." She watched the rector wipe his hands and she resolved to have more private words with Julia.

From the platform at the far side of the grass, music began to fill the meadow. The musicians had started to rehearse. A lilting tune floated to the tops of the surrounding trees. Upon this enchanting scene stepped the Witton girls.

Oglesby gaped at them, his jaw dropping in astonishment. All of the sisters were dressed in identical fairy costumes. Their hair was covered by filmy scarfs and wreaths of small blue forget-me-nots, and their faces were hidden by masks edged in lace. The white gowns they wore were of flowing, diaphanous batiste caught up by golden cords of silk across their bosoms. They looked like sprites venturing out upon the meadow.

Quoting from the Bible, Oglesby said, "'This is Jezebel.'" His eyes searched for a clue to which young lady was his intended.

"My dear bishop," Amanda cried, "look what they have done. Now no one will be capable of telling them apart. 'Tis too vexing." She marched up to her daughters. "At least I know which is Sarah," she said to the shortest of the four.

"Oh, Mama," Sarah wailed. "Why did you give me away?"

"I have my duty to uphold as your mother, young lady." She draped her shawl over Sarah's shoulders, which were nearly bare due to the classic Grecian style of her gown. "Do not forget you will be retiring a good deal earlier than your sisters."

Sarah did not reply. She merely kicked the ground with the toe of her slipper.

"I hope we have not displeased you too greatly, Mama," Faith said in a low voice. "You see, this is our last lark together before Julia goes away with Mr. Oglesby. We have been planning it for an age."

"Marion?" Amanda peered at the speaker.

Her daughters broke into giggles.

"We shall not tell you who is who, Mama." Julia spoke in the same low voice as Faith. She looked about. "Where is Lord Rossiter?"

The bishop came forward, leaving the rector to continue gaping. "He has some important papers to write up before he joins us. He shall be along later." He grinned at his daughters, which caused them to think he had mayhap taken leave of his senses. "Very fetching frocks you're wearing, my dears. Try not to embarrass our guests with this charade." He offered his arm to Amanda. They went off to their post under the garland arch leading into the meadow.

The Witton sisters became aware of Oglesby's fixed regard. "Whatever can the matter be with Mr. Oglesby?" Marion asked in an aside.

With eyes opened so wide that more white than pale grey showed, and with his chin jutting to an abnormal extension, Oglesby staggered forward, coming to a trembling halt. He tottered a moment, too overcome to speak. Then his words spilled out in a gush of anguish. "My dear Miss Witton—whichever the one you are—how could you display yourself with such a want of modesty for all the world to see? A fairy! Of all the heathenish creatures to portray. I thank Providence that neither my uncle, the Bishop of Durham, nor any of my parishioners are here to see your shame."

"Who wants that pack of posturing bores," muttered Sarah.

His eyes dwelled upon the exposed shoulders of the young ladies. "This sort of dress is all very well for an actress, but for the daughters of clergy it is hardly the thing. No, I cannot approve! And I order you, Miss Witton—whichever the one you are—to change your raiment before the guests arrive. I will not stand for this want of delicacy."

Three of the fairies stared at the one standing indignantly in their midst.

"Let me speak for my sister Julia," said Julia, her voice low and angry. "If I were she, I would not obey such a command. No man should order a woman's life to the degree that he tells her what she may or may not wear."

Oglesby's eyes narrowed. "Miss Marion? Let me tell you, young miss, that it ill befits you to speak thus to a man of the cloth."

"Oh?" Marion said, standing one sister away from Julia.

The rector glanced from one sister to the next. "Miss Sarah," he said, coming up to the shortest, "I demand that you tell me which sister is which."

A mischievous smile crept over Sarah's lips. She stepped away from the others. "Well, now, shall we have a look?" She walked up and down before her elder siblings, then turned to the rector. "They look remarkably alike, do they not?" She shook her head. "By my soul, I do not think I can do it. Can you tell them apart, Mr. Oglesby?"

"This is madness!" He lunged forward to grab the mask of one of the fairies. They all darted away from him. "By heaven, Miss Witton, when we are wed I shall not countenance this sort of behaviour. You will obey my every word. 'Spare the rod and spoil the child.' That goes for wives as well, my dear bride." He moved toward one of the girls, but she fled from him. "Come here this instant!"

"But, Mr. Oglesby, during Midsummer Eve, lovers are supposed to play games with each other." Sarah smiled ingenuously at the rector. "'Jack shall have Jill; naught will go ill.' Oh dear! But your first name isn't Jack, is it?" She bit her lips, playing the mindless innocent.

"By all the angels in heaven, Miss Sarah, you shall live to regret your iniquitous behaviour." Snorting, he stalked off in the direction of the table laden with kegs of ale and cider. As he crossed a stretch of uneven grass, his nose pointing to the sky, the rector tripped and fell on his face like a dropped cane.

The young ladies started forward, but stopped when he regained his footing in his curious, stiff-jointed fashion. They buried their laughter in their hands when his gaze slid their way. With marked purpose he marched to the footman pouring out the ale.

"Oh, Julia," Faith said, then sighed, "I wish you were about to marry a *real* man. Someone who would whisk you off your feet, instead of getting whisked off his own."

Marion looked at the group of guests entering under the arch. "I wonder if Harry will come."

"He'll come," Julia replied tightly. "He promised."

The meadow soon filled with costumed guests, all set upon a night of revelry. Mrs. Witton was sure that some of the local countryfolk had managed to blend in with the gentry and peerage. The invited hundred guests had swollen somehow to a number far exceeding what was expected. It was ever thus when one held a masked gathering alfresco.

The lively fairies made their mark upon the guests. They offered to cast spells and foretell whom one would marry. The spirit of nonsense that poured forth from the bishop's daughters was taken up by the rest of the company. Soon the meadow was filled with harmless cavorting and merrymaking.

Upon this frolicsome scene strolled Harry. His red domino covered him to his feet. A floppy plumed hat hid his face.

A fairy ran up to him, lifting the skirt of her flowing gown to keep from tripping, and thus revealing a trim ankle. There was something quite familiar about her.

"Harry," she murmured when she reached his side.

His senses tingled at her low voice. He looked at her quizzically. "Julia?"

A throaty laugh greeted his query. "If you meet me at the Trysting Place at midnight, perhaps then I'll tell you who I am." A wide grin stretched delightfully across her lips.

"Faith? Marion?"

The fairy laughed again, then reached up and placed a warm kiss on the corner of his mouth. She fled before the stunned Harry could respond.

He made after her, but she disappeared into the crowd of dancers. As Harry turned to push his way out of the press of guests, he encountered another fairy dressed exactly like the one who had just vanished in the opposite direction.

"Thunder and turf!" He grabbed the young lady away from her partner. "What is the meaning of this? Julia?"

His question was met with a low laugh—one remarkably like the laugh he had heard just moments earlier from the other fairy.

"Sir, I am dancing with the young lady," her partner said. "Be off and find another to suit you."

"A moment, please," the fairy said to her escort, then turned to Harry.

"A sprite, dressed like you, just kissed me." The major moved closer trying to see through the lace that covered most of her face. "Were you the one?"

"She kissed you! By all that's wonderful, is that not grand. Oh, Harry, I am happy for you—no matter which one of us it was."

"Faith? Marion? Blast, tell me who you are!"

The girl wagged a finger at him. "I cannot." Her partner came to her and they resumed the dance.

Harry scraped off his hat and ran his hand through his hair. His eyes narrowed. Feeling a tap on his shoulder, he turned to encounter yet another fairy. This one was noticeably shorter than the other two. He caught the girl's hand.

"Harry, would you dance with me? Mama said she would allow me a few dances if you or Father partnered me." Sarah hung her head. "She caught me dancing with Tristan Kimball and chided me so for wanton behaviour. I shan't be officially out until forever."

"I should be honoured to take a turn with you, but first tell me which sister is which."

Sarah's eyes widened. "Can't you tell? Harry, you have known them for an age. I would never have taken you for a gudgeon."

"I must know, Sarah, please."

"But I cannot tell you. We took an oath not to reveal our identities to anyone, not even Father and Mama. Of course, Mama knew me at once." She held out her hand to him. "My dance, Harry?"

He took her hand and bowed formally over it. "Forgive my lack of manners, dear lady. Only the press of affairs keeps me from claiming the privilege of leading you out. The set after this shall be ours." He grinned at her. "Now, come down from the boughs, little love. I shall return for you, never fear. Just stay away from the Kimball lad. A wild one, my pixie, who will leave you with nothing but pages and pages to read about prudence and virtue."

With a look of resignation, Sarah said, "I already have thirty pages to read for tomorrow from Mr. Hobson's *Sermons and Essays*." She glanced about and spied her parents close by. "Sometimes I feel as if I am still in leading-strings."

"'Tis a pity these days that our young ladies go from leading-strings to harnesses," Harry observed. He began to take his leave. Sarah touched his arm and said, "Are you looking for one of my sisters?" Her smile was answered by his. "Which one?"

His smile turned to a self-mocking grin. "I wish I knew."

"Which one do you want?"

The question set his mind in motion as he turned and made his way through the crowd.

Once across the meadow, Harry continued his pursuit, his attention so caught up that he gave no thought to where he went. He stepped back and collided with someone.

"Easy there, major." A pair of strong hands kept Harry from stumbling.

Major Druce turned and encountered a character out of the pages of history. A buccaneer, who looked to have just landed from a long sojourn in the Indies, stood before him. From the wide-brimmed black hat to the boots covering most of his legs, the man looked the part of a swash-buckling adventurer. The dagger thrust under his sash gave one a feeling of being at a disadvantage. Since the man wore no mask, save for his silver patch, he was easily recognized.

"Fine looking rig, Rossiter," Harry said.

"Do you like it? My man will be so pleased. He went to great lengths to procure it." Rossiter turned his wrist so that the fall of lace tumbled in rather pretty folds. "I find these demned sleeves a nuisance." He held a billowing sleeve away from his leather jerkin.

Harry muttered an incoherent remark.

"Just so. Would you believe that my valet, usually a sensible fellow, tried to persuade me to come dressed as a Roman? Now, I ask you, what man of taste would wish to go about in a sheet? Demned things flap embarrassingly in the breeze."

Clapping the pirate on the shoulder, Harry said, grinning, "You made a wise choice. By the by, have you seen any fair nymphs roaming about lately?"

"Blister it, fellow, I've seen three—no, four! Most confusing."

"I am looking for only one out of the four."

"Look no further man, for here one comes."

A fairy came toward them, then paused. She looked at Rossiter, from his hat set cavalierly at an angle to his shirt, lying open at the neck, down to his boots hugging his thighs. Her gaze travelled back up him and met his eye.

"Ah, Lord Pirate and gallant stranger," she said in a low voice, moving closer to the gentlemen. "Shall I tell your fortunes?"

Harry advanced upon the young lady. "I have been looking everywhere for you," he whispered. "What did you mean by kissing me, then running off like that?"

A cautious attitude manifested itself upon the girl's half-hidden countenance. "I am shy," she suggested.

"Faith?" Harry asked in a puzzled voice.

"But, my dear masked one, are you so sure that I am the one named Faith?" She kept her voice low.

"I have had enough of this charade! I shall see you now, not later at the oak." Harry grabbed for her mask.

Rossiter's hand shot out and caught Harry's before the major could reveal her face. "It is not time yet for the unmasking."

The fairy took Harry's hand from the pirate's firm grasp. She turned his hand over and examined the palm. She looked at him, then gazed up at the stars.

"You are a military man," she murmured. "An officer, I think. You have been very brave in battle. But you are about to claim a great victory in the age-old struggle of man and woman. I beseech you be patient." By her stance she conveyed her entreaty. "Would you humour my wishes and meet me—later?"

He gripped her hand. "Do not fail to be at the Trysting Place. For, believe me, my happiness depends upon you. I shall wish the time to fly. Till midnight then."

She leaned forward and kissed Harry on the chin. "Are you so sure I am the one?" Her tone was compassionate. "Until midnight, dear friend," she said, stepping away.

With a puzzled expression, Harry strode off.

Rossiter moved to her side. "Ah, my charming wood nymph," he said, taking her hand in his, "I desire that you cast a spell over me, besides the spell of your beauty."

"You, Lord Pirate, desire a spell, do you?" She faced him. "What sort did you have in mind—warts, boils or dyspepsia?"

"A spell, not a hex, kind minx. You see, for the longest time—nigh unto a sennight—I have been plagued by this stubborn woman."

"Oh? She is stubborn?"

"Yes, I am afraid 'tis true. Try as I may to convince her that the course she follows will only bring her grief, still she continues with her ill-conceived scheme. Was there ever a more obdurate female?" He kissed her hand. "Now, winsome fairy, I wish you to cast a spell. A love spell so powerful that when this lady sees me, she will be so taken that all thoughts of a walking-stick parson will flee her mind, and she shall think only of a one-eyed pirate."

She turned from Thomas. "You want a love spell?"

"Yes, Julia, I do." He placed his hands upon her shoulder.

She stilled at his touch. "You knew it was I?" she asked in a whisper.

"How can one not know one's own heart?"

"Confess, Thomas, you merely guessed." Her tone became pragmatic.

"Blister it, madam, are you a sprite or a shrew?" He turned her to face him. "A man cannot get very far in his courting if the lady concerned will not take his advances seriously."

"A man of your repute oughtn't be taken too seriously."

"Gad, Julia, that's a killing thrust. My repute, as you call it, has been much exaggerated."

"Then you don't name species of flowers after opera dancers in your keeping?"

"Where the devil did you hear that story?"

"Marion had it on authority from one of her dearest friends. Do you deny it?" She gazed at him with a hopeful expression. Her eyes wandered from the amused look on his face down to his open shirt-front. A man should not have such a mass of hair on his chest. It was quite distracting.

"No," he said, "I cannot deny it. But it was long ago, when I was a greenhorn." He moved away with an impatient step. "The locals must be dipping deep to come up with that bit of gossip."

She looked conscience-stricken. "It was wrong to listen to such talk. But...Thomas, I scarcely know you. One moment you are Lord Rossiter, stylish gentleman of the ton and—", she smiled "—scholar of botany. The next instant you are a charmer, a pirate, a thorough rogue. Your *bona fides* are left in grave doubt, sir."

"But do *you* doubt me?"

"I...I do not know."

"Then I'll not rush you, my girl, even with your wedding fast approaching. Just trust me, please. At times, I admit, I am not what I appear to be. Yet, there is rhyme and reason to all this mad business."

She quietly gazed at him for a long moment. "Perhaps after the unmasking we will know each other better." She turned to watch her father carry a torch to the pile of wood. The bishop made a brief speech and then lit the bonfire.

"'Tis midnight," Thomas observed. "The unmasking begins." He turned around to find his nymph had fled into the woods. Only a flutter of white could he see as the lady disappeared in the direction of the Trysting Place.

CHAPTER TWELVE

"HARRY," JULIA CALLED as she neared the old oak. "Harry?" She stood in the clearing, her hands on her hips. The fine drapery of her gown floated in the gentle breeze. Fiercely she whispered his name again as she scanned the area.

The serenity of the Trysting Place remained unbroken. Even the merrymaking in the nearby meadow did not intrude on the quiet of the clearing. There was only the whisper of the wind in the tree tops, like lovers murmuring. Where was Harry?

Unbeknownst to Julia, a man sat at the base of a tree a few paces from where she stood, screened from her view by bushes. He was whittling a piece of wood with a long knife. Between his legs a small pile of shavings grew with each silent movement of his knife.

He had stayed close to the major for most of the evening, just as he had been ordered to. He knew from overheard conversations that he was in the right place, that his vigil would be rewarded.

His knife stilled at the call of a nightingale. Answering back as a whippoorwill, he paused a moment before resuming his whittling. Though occupied with the piece of wood, he listened to every sound as he kept guard over the spinney.

On the other side of the clearing, by the footpath leading to Lovers' Walk, a pair of men crept into the underbrush and began to reconnoitre the area. Their cover was sparse, but sufficient in the darkness for their purpose. They crouched behind a leafy bush, communicating with their hands. The gestures of one man became quite wild and quick, Gallic in nature. He subsided at the sounds of someone coming along the path.

Julia stopped her pacing. Turning at the footfall behind her, she again put her hands on her hips. "What kept you?"

"Harry?" a disbelieving voice asked, as it came closer. A mirror image of Julia stepped forward to face her. "What are *you* doing here?"

"I came to meet Harry."

"But *I'm* meeting him! You go away."

"My business with him is quite important. I would not be here if it were not."

"Oh, Julia, how could you? You shall ruin everything!"

Julia glared at her sister. "Do you think I am doing this to ruin your plans? Only a matter of...utmost urgency could force me to come between a sister and the man she loves."

"Urgency? What a bouncer!"

At the soft curse from the direction of the footpath, the sisters fell silent for a moment.

"'Tis Harry. Julia, do go away!"

"I cannot."

From the darkness surrounding the clearing, Harry's caped figure emerged and moved swiftly forward. He stopped at the sight of *two* masked fairies waiting for him. "What the blazes is this? Have you girls been making a jest of me?"

His angry voice caused one sister to moan and hide herself behind the other. "I knew this would happen if you stayed," she said, laying the blame at Julia's feet.

"Harry, don't be a paperscull. I had to talk to you about—" Julia paused and glanced back at her sister "—about the papers," she whispered to Harry as she removed her mask.

"Blast you, Julia!" He threw off his own mask. "What the hell do I care about those blasted papers? They've been nothing but trouble since you told me about them." He grabbed her arm. "Now, get out of the way. You are coming between a man and—", his voice softened "—his destiny." He moved Julia to the side and looked at the girl left standing before him. "Marion?"

Her downcast head shot up. "You knew?"

"I hoped," he said, taking her hand in his. He pulled her to him, then tugged on the ribbons securing her mask until it fell at their feet.

"You hoped it would be me?" Marion asked, her voice filling with wonder.

"I wanted it to be you," he murmured, as he held her closer.

Julia cleared her throat.

Harry raised his lips from Marion's. "Julia, go away." He reclaimed the sweet mouth trembling inches from his.

Turning her back to them, Julia said, "This cannot wait any longer. For days I have tried to have a moment alone with you. Between Oglesby and Lord Rossiter I've had the devil of a time. Harry?"

He raised his head. "In a moment." Marion wound her arms more tightly around his neck. "In a few moments," he amended.

Julia sighed in exasperation and moved away from the couple to the other side of the clearing. She failed to notice the bush just in front of her swayed slightly, as the two it concealed crawled back into the brush.

The man sitting by the tree was more attentive. He saw the movement. At the soft call of a nightingale nearby he looked around, then relaxed when his leader appeared before him. He gazed up lazily from his comfortable spot on the ground, motioned with his knife to the opposite side of the clearing and raised two fingers. A gleam of silver acknowledged the message.

Across the spinney, Julia walked back and forth as she counted to a hundred. She glanced over at Harry and Marion, heaved a noisy sigh and began counting again.

On her third set of hundreds, she lost patience. She tromped over to the couple. "If you are going to carry on in such a way, Harry Druce, you had better speak to our father and pay your formal addresses."

The lovers reluctantly drew apart. Marion murmured something and held on to Harry's arm. He glowered at Julia, then turned back to Marion. Raising her hand to his lips, he said, "Would you wait for me in the summer-house, my love? I shall join you there when I've settled this business with Julia. Then later, you and I will seek your father out for his blessing. You *will* marry me, won't you, Marion?"

Julia glanced up in disbelief. "Don't be a cluck! Of course she'll marry you!"

The couple glared at her.

"We shall talk again," Harry said to Marion. "When we won't always be interrupted." He gently pushed her in the direction of Lovers' Walk. "I shall be with you in a little, my love." He watched Marion leave, then turned to Julia. "Well?"

She retreated a step from the furious look in his eyes. "Well indeed! I shall remember not to come visiting during your first year of marriage. I can see you two will want to be alone."

He grinned. "We will. And if you could just pass the word along to the other relations, I should be much obliged."

"I envy you two—the promise of the future before you, the happiness of being together, and so full of love. I wish I might..." She shook her head, as if trying to dispel the images that crowded her mind. Unbidden, her thoughts had turned to Thomas. She wondered what sort of husband he might make. The notion of the silver-patched devil ever marrying was ridiculous, of course. He seemed to enjoy the variety of the garden too much to settle for just one bloom. A wistful smile touched her lips.

"What do you have to smile about?" Harry asked. "If I were a woman facing the prospect of settling into a life with Oglesby, I would go into a full decline."

"I have already tried that. It did not work. Besides, I did not come here to discuss that bothersome man. What about the pouch? Did you find anyone who knows anything about it?"

Harry walked slowly up to her. In a low, tightly controlled voice, he said, "If you ever ask another favour of me, I shall quite happily wring your demned neck. Never in my life have I been subjected to such a number of quizzical stares and lifted eyebrows, not even after this." He raised his half-empty sleeve. "Every chap I asked said, Flowers? Then gave me such a look that I wished I could crawl down between the flagstones." He held out his hand. "I want you to give the pouch over to me."

"I cannot! Do you suppose I carry it about with me? What sort of bird-witted female do you take me for?"

"The sort that has no compunction about using a friend in the most shameless manner. Now, give me the pouch, Julia!"

"No! Why should I?"

"Because you are in danger." He gazed at her in a measured way. "I received a letter today from my colonel—about the pouch."

"From your colonel? Well, what did he say?"

Harry ran his hand over the nape of his neck. "Colonel Murray's instructions were specific—I was to obey the orders enclosed with his letter." He thrust his hand under the red domino and pulled out a folded sheet of paper, which he handed to Julia.

She moved into a shaft of moonlight, which illuminated the sheet, enabling her to read it. The scrawled message was to the point. "'You will be contacted by me—the owner of the pouch,'" she said, reading the missive aloud. "'Get the papers from Miss Witton. Hold them until I make myself known to you. I am called the Tulip. Give the pouch only to me.'" She looked up. "Harry, this message is signed with a Tulip, the same one as on the packet."

"I thought it might be. We're in a wretched fix, dear girl. Someone knows you have those blasted papers."

Her gaze met his. She made a helpless movement with her hands. "How could anyone possibly know? You are the only one I've told." She closed her eyes and rubbed her forehead, as if bidding her thoughts to come more quickly. "Lord Rossiter.... Could he have come here to get the papers? He claimed I had something of his."

"Rossiter! Come now, Julia. Granted, at one time he was thought of quite highly. Something of a hero even. But now... Got his nose all day in books, and if the gossip is to be believed, at night he's, ah, doing field research with the aid of some fair bud of delight. He is hardly what one would look for in a spy.''

Harry's words gave her pause. Was Thomas a spy? The man was an interesting choice, if so. He wore a silver patch, which she knew he had no use for other than ornamentation; or was it to disguise his appearance. He posed as a fop, yet in her company his manner was far from foppish. But a spy?

"I know not what to think," she said, stepping impatiently away.

"What you think doesn't give me cause for concern. What worries me is what you'll *do*." Harry moved to Julia and took her by the arm. "If you take some strange notion into your head and land in the suds, by jingo, I'll wring your neck. Julia, you must promise me that you won't do anything, anything at all, about the pouch. Promise?"

"But—"

"Promise!"

She gave him an angry look. "Very well, I give my word not to do anything until I have informed you first. Satisfied?"

"No. I'll not be easy until I have given the pouch to the courier. I know your tricks. The knowledge has kept me awake on more than one night."

"You wretch, one would think I was your foe. I am your friend. Soon to be your sister, but not if you keep Marion waiting much longer."

He glanced back in the direction of Lovers' Walk. "I hope she's still at the summer-house."

"She will be. She's not a paperscull like you. Now go," she said, giving him a nudge forward.

"Remember your promise!" As she nodded grudgingly, Harry strode from the Trysting Place.

Julia looked down as she brought the Tulip's missive from between the folds of her gown. She held it up to the moonlight to read it again. Looking at the drawing of the flower, she wondered if she could keep her word to Harry.

Rossiter watched her as she read the note over. A satisfied smile played upon his lips, causing the corner of his mouth to quirk up. He motioned to Scully, indicating the man should stay put. Then Thomas rose quietly and walked to the path leading into the spinney. Barely making a sound, he moved to within arm's reach of Julia.

"Ah, reading a *billet-doux* from your betrothed, the worthy Atley Oglesby?"

She jumped at the first sound of his voice. "You!" She glanced down at the paper in her hand and tucked it into the bodice of her gown. "You gave me quite a start." She looked up at him with more interest. "Where did you come from?"

"I have come on the wings of my heart, my fairy queen, from a kingdom close at hand, yet seldom seen by mere mortals."

"Are you foxed?"

"I am befuddled with the wine of your beauty."

She glanced heavenward and sighed. "Thomas, do you not get exhausted thinking up all these flowery speeches?"

He rocked forward, as if not quite stable in his balance or quite clear in his eyesight. "I find thinking of you invigorating, not fatiguing at all." He caressed her hand. "'Come, my queen, take hands with me,' as Oberon said. 'Now thou and I are new in amity.'"

"Why is it I feel you are making sport of me?" She peered at him, a suspicious glint in her eyes, and softly asked, "Thomas, what sort of game are you engaged in?"

"Won't you trust me, my queen, and play my game, if only for tonight?" His lips moved into a seductive smile.

An answering twinkle lurked in her eyes. "What is it you would have me play, milord?"

He reeled against her like a drunken man and threw an arm around her shoulders. "You are my queen, the fair Titania, and I am your lord, Oberon, King of the Fairies." He coaxed her steps forward. "We will away!" With his arm about her, he pulled her along to the footpath. Planting a resounding kiss near her ear, he glanced at the bush that shook, without the aid of the wind, and the gloved hand that stilled its movement. Thomas hid his grin as he murmured something outrageous to Julia.

"You are besotted all right! But with Father's ale, not with my 'tempting white bosom.'" She put her arm about his waist and led him along to Lovers' Walk. She nearly fell over when he leaned upon her shoulder. "I would never have thought you could become so castaway, Thomas, and in so short a time."

He grinned down at her. "My name, fair Titania, is Oberon. Pray remember it."

"Well, Oberon, you shall have to sober a bit if you wish to stay in my company. Here, sit and take a few deep breaths." She led him to a fallen log and helped him sit down. "Breathe in, breathe out. That always clears Lucian's head when it is a bit worse for the wine."

"Lucian?"

"My brother, the one who is in Portugal."

He raised his hand in a feigned toast. "Here's to all our brave lads fighting for King and country. May Providence guide them and bring 'em home safe. God bless 'em!" He brought his hand to his lips and made groping movements for the liquid that was not there.

Julia pulled his hand away from his mouth. "You have celebrated enough for one night. Now, breathe in and out."

He let out a gust of air and pulled her down beside him on the log. "That's better." He leaned his head on her shoulder. "Fair Titania, how many children shall we have?" His head nearly parted company with his neck as she jerked away.

"Fairies don't have children!"

"Of course they do. How else do you think so many of 'em came to be? As king and queen, we must do our duty."

She struck her fist to her thigh. "Why must you remind me of duty at a time like this? Duty! I am sick of the word. 'Tis duty that got me into this hubble-bubble."

He took her hand and stroked it. "And it was duty that brought me here to you."

She looked at him. Her mind wandered back to the pouch. "Thomas, what do you know about tulips?"

"Tulips?" He glanced at her with a quizzical smile. "A genus of Eurasian bulbous herbs of the lily family. Mostly grown for their showy flowers."

"Can you sketch?"

"My sire insisted on my instruction in all of the arts and sciences. My tutor, however, informed me that I was the merest dabbler, and that I should not aspire to the heights of Gainsborough."

Her brows inched up in a sceptical manner. "What were you occupied in doing a sennight ago, early in the morning before dawn?"

He smiled dreamily. "A wood nymph. I was pursuing a wood nymph." His smile broadened as he leaned over and kissed her on the lips.

She drew back and swallowed as she put her hand on his chest, touching the fringe of crisp hair escaping from his open shirt. Her quickening heartbeat pounded in her ears. Her mind seemed to lose direction. She wanted only to feel. "Would you do that again?" She leaned toward him.

Thomas put his arms around her, but held her a little away from him. "A gentleman does not take advantage of a lady who is betrothed to another."

"A wise man once said, 'At times one must transcend the proprieties.' Besides, you are not a gentleman, but a king. I'm not a lady, but Queen of the Fairies." Her hand crept up to tease the corner of his mouth. "You may kiss me, Oberon."

Slowly he brought his lips to hers. The fire of their kiss set her senses aflame. She pulled closer to him. He seemed unwilling to rush her to unexplored realms of pleasure until she had savoured fully the simple delights at hand. His kisses were unhurried, light yet somehow painfully intense. His lips moved from hers and wandered to her ear. She thought she heard him murmur, "Julia, I must have you."

"What . . . what did you say?" she whispered.

He tucked her head beneath his chin, as his fingers stroked her neck and jaw. "I was merely wishing Oglesby to Jericho."

She silently echoed his sentiments. It was surprising how frequently they shared the same thoughts, especially concerning the rector.

Thomas put her away from him, stood and held out his hand. "Would you walk with me?"

"Walk? Now?"

"A lady with your propensity for odd behaviour in the moonlight oughtn't question another's impulse. There is something I must put to the test. Come."

She rose to her feet and strolled at Thomas's side down the path. Taking her hand, he tucked it into the crook of his arm, and they walked slowly by the meadow, where the night's revelry was at its height.

"I daresay we ought to return to the others." Though she said it, she did not mean it.

"Not just yet."

When at last they came to the end of Lovers' Walk, Thomas turned to face her, bringing her hand to his lips.

"Rossiter, what are you up to? You have acted in a most curious manner since we left the Trysting Place."

"Ah, yes, the Trysting Place. That is where sweethearts meet, is it not?"

"Yes."

"You believe in legends, don't you, Julia?" He took both of her hands in his and held them to his chest.

She stepped back, looking at him in a puzzled way. "Thomas—"

"Remember, for tonight I am Oberon."

He looked more like an adventurer than a mythical forest creature. Yet, for now she would play his game.

"Do you believe, my queen?"

"Long ago I believed in legends, fairy tales and happy-ever-afters." She gazed at her hands in his. "I want to believe again. But there is so very much in the way, keeping me from the magic. Mr. Oglesby—"

"Forget about the rector for a time. This moment is between you and me. We have come down Lovers' Walk together." He clasped her hands more tightly. "Do you know what the legend says will occur now?"

At that moment, the legend had little power to move her compared to the wonder-workings of his presence. She only wished that legends were true, so that the enchantment of the night would go on forever. But because she was a practical lady, reality dashed her senses like a dousing of cold water.

"Thomas, are you trying to compromise me? Hoax me with talk of legends?" She pulled out of his grasp. "I am betrothed. Promised to—"

"A man you despise. Come, it is high time to call off this ridiculous farce of an engagement. Tell your father that you cannot marry Oglesby."

"I have tried to tell him. 'Twas useless. Mr. Oglesby is considered a suitable match. If I cannot persuade the rector to cry off, then I shall have to wed him."

"The devil you will! I won't stand by and watch you throw yourself away."

"You can do nothing to stop me."

He looked at her with a wicked smile that became wider and wider. Then he threw back his head and laughed, with his hands braced on his hips in an insolent fashion. Never had he looked more like a buccaneer.

Overcoming his mirth, Thomas walked around Julia as if sizing up his challenge. "So there is nothing I can do to stop you, hey? My dear girl—" he took her in his arms "—how little you know me." He drew her close and began to better their acquaintance.

"I say," Oglesby declared, his words slurred, as he came upon them in their embrace, "that's my betrothed you've got your arms about, sirrah." He tottered nearer. Reeling from the effects of too much ale, the rector staggered into the pair, treading on Julia's toe.

"Ouch!" She began to hop on one foot.

"Let that be a lesson to you, Rosh, er, Rossiter!" Try as he might, Oglesby could not bring his eyes to focus upon his lordship, and his betrothed seemed to weave before his eyes. "I shall take great pleasure in thrashing you as you deserve, you dog. 'Course I knew the girl had more experience than she was letting on to. I haven't known many girls as old as she is who are still as pure as they pretend to be. Not that I blame you for dallying with her. She ish a delightsome armful."

As she heard sounds of impotent fury come from behind her, Julia instinctively put her arms out to restrain Thomas.

"Stand aside, Julia, before I move you. That pimple-headed simpleton will pay for his drunken talk."

"I shay!" Oglesby let loose a fine spray with his words. "No need to become insulting, Rossiter, ol' friend. We men understand the frail ways of women. Half of 'em are sluts and the other half ain't worth taking to bed. Now, my Miss Witton here, she promises to be a pleasure worth savoring, every morsel of her." He leered at her and licked his wet lips.

Julia drew a deep breath and stepped aside. She turned to Thomas. "Thrash him," she commanded, pointing to Oglesby. "If you won't, I shall!"

"There's no cause to get huffy," Oglesby retorted. Espying Julia's derrière, he gave it a slap.

Thomas, fists clenched, moved swiftly past Julia. At the sight of the charging lord, Oglesby staggered back and tripped. "This is an outrage! Knocking down a man of God ain't to be tolerated." He tried to get up, but fell flat on his back. "You, sirrah, are no gentleman! Striking a man before he's had a chance to gain his footing is . . . shabby, is what it is."

Looking from his unused fists to the man sprawled out in the dirt before him, Thomas began to chuckle. "Mr. Oglesby, I must crave your pardon."

"You must?" Julia looked in disbelief at Thomas.

"Most assuredly." Rossiter hauled the rector up from the ground. "A man of your position deserves more than this—much more." Roughly dusting the fellow off,

Thomas propelled him toward the manor house garden. Julia followed, lifting her skirts to keep up with them. "A man of your sort," Thomas continued, hurrying Oglesby along with his long strides, "out of the ordinary from anyone in humankind, should receive the rewards he solicits so arduously. I hope that my treatment of you a few moments ago was not taken amiss?"

Oglesby's feet were barely touching the ground. Rossiter was urging him on by grasping the seat of his breeches and the collar of his black coat. On they went to the centre of the garden.

"Nothing to be taken amiss, milord," the rector said, looking a bit bemused by his rate of travel. "Men of the world, such as you and I, understand a fellow's impetuosity in the heat of the moment."

"Then I know you will understand the impetuosity of this moment." So saying, Thomas heaved Oglesby head first into the fish-pond.

"Well done!" Julia clapped Thomas on the back as she enjoyed the sight of the flailing, splashing cleric. "You don't think he's drowning, do you? The water is no more than a foot deep."

"He looks to be swimming to me."

Oglesby came up from his face-down position, spurting a mouthful of water. His arms ceased their flapping motion as he pushed himself up. But the slick bottom of the pond made him lose his hold and he went under again.

"Someone ought to pull him out," observed Julia. "Can one be a widow before being a bride?"

"An interesting question. One that ought to be pondered thoroughly. However, I really think Oglesby is running out of air." He looked down at his own handsome leather boots and sighed regretfully. Placing a foot gingerly into the water, Thomas pushed back the lace at his wrist and yanked the rector up by the scruff of the neck.

Oglesby blinked as he emitted a stream of water from his mouth. He gasped for air. "What happened? Did I fall in?"

Julia and Thomas exchanged a look.

"Mr. Oglesby," she said, as if scolding a child, "this is dreadful. Lord Rossiter, how could you be so clumsy? Just look what you have done."

"I apologize, sir. Ruined your cravat." Thomas peered closely at the sodden mess dangling from the rector's neck. "Demned shame."

Oglesby sneezed, spraying the pair before him.

"You are catching a chill." Julia dabbed the mist from her face.

With a fastidiousness that would have done the finest of the fashionable set proud, Thomas dried the moisture from his own cheeks. "Must get you out those wet clothes," he said to the rector. "Not at all the thing to be seen looking like a drowned rat. You might even contract an inflammation of the lungs."

"One can only hope," Julia said, then after a pause added, "that no lasting malady lingers."

"Come along, worthy parson." Thomas took Oglesby warily by the arm. "I shall have my man find you something to wear. The fit will be a disgrace, you being less in stature than I, but, my dear fellow, you cannot possibly desire to be seen in that dripping rig." The two men began to move slowly to the house. Glancing back over his shoulder, Thomas raised his patch and winked at Julia.

"I'll join the others and wait for you in the meadow," she called to him.

Only a moment after the men had disappeared from her view, Julia became aware of a shadowy figure moving toward her from the back of the garden. She made ready to follow Thomas, for she had no wish to fend off a drunken guest alone.

"*Excusez-moi, mademoiselle*," the man called, as she took a few steps away from him. "I must speak to you, Miss Witton."

Julia turned to face the man. He was draped in a black domino, with the hood drawn over his head like a monk. Her instincts told her to go, but still she held her ground.

"Miss Witton." He bowed. "I have come to claim my pouch."

CHAPTER THIRTEEN

JULIA TRIED to keep the surprise from showing on her face. She peered at the man, but the darkness hid his features.

"You have it, do you not?" he asked.

The intensity in his voice alarmed her. She answered him in a cautious manner. "That would depend on what pouch you mean, sir, and who you are. I do not know you."

"No, I am a stranger to you. Yet I can satisfy your well-founded suspicions. I am an agent for your most bountiful government."

"But you are a Frenchman." She edged carefully away from him.

"Have no fear, Miss Witton. I did not come to harm you, but only to take back that which is mine. Surely you would not deny me the possession of what is rightfully mine?" He stepped closer.

"What is your name, sir?"

"For the present, you may address me merely as Philippe. My identity must be kept secret, you see. Let me assure you, *mademoiselle*, that I am a loyal servant of the Crown. That Bonaparte!" He spat on the ground. "He has befouled my country. I help to rid France of his odious presence by working for my good friends, the British."

"Oh?"

"*Oui*, that is so. It is not enough for me to sit here placidly on your welcome shores and enjoy the benevolence of you kind English." He shook his head. "*Non, non*, I would reclaim what is rightfully mine. To do this I must bring about the downfall of the one who dares call himself Emperor!'' Philippe calmed himself. ''I do my little part. But now I have failed.'' He drew nearer. ''I must have that pouch.''

She sidestepped him, moving closer to the house. ''How did you come to lose the packet, *monsieur*?''

''Ah! You test me. This is good. There are many who want the papers in it. It is good that you question me, and anyone else who asks you about it. Do not give it up easily. It would be a *désastre* if the papers fell into the hands of the enemy.''

To Julia, the man sounded more dramatic with each sentence he uttered, as if he were playing at being the zealous Royalist. An adept player of parts herself, she recognized when someone was trying to hoodwink her. Why was this man, this Philippe, going to such lengths to convince her of his veracity? Was he what he claimed to be?

''Again I ask you, *monsieur*, how did you lose the pouch you speak of?''

He looked at her closely. ''Ah, you are a lady of singular persistence. Not many of your gentle sex would have the presence of mind to stay with a question for more than a moment. How unusual you are, *mademoiselle*. But this cheers me. I would not like something of such value to be in the hands of a feeble-minded woman.''

''The pouch, sir?''

''Ah, I digress. Many nights ago, I was on my way to the south coast to leave for France, taking the new plans for my men with me. Riders began to chase my coach. I knew they were after the papers in the pouch I carried. Rather than let these men take the plans from me, I risked throwing them out the window. Later, after dealing with my pursuers, I planned to return for the packet. If the worst befell me, the papers would not be found. But they were found, were they not, dear lady?"

"Perhaps."

"Ah, you remain unconvinced. Shall I describe the pouch to you?"

"If you wish."

Philippe stroked his chin as he gazed at her thoughtfully. This lady was of a most unyielding nature. She did not mould to his will like the others of her gender did. She had a fire of her own that made her independent of his own magnificent heat. This woman did not need a man to give life to her existence, only one to enhance it. How odd she was, and how impatient she was getting with him, which was oddest of all.

In a confiding tone he described to her the markings of the tulip on the pouch and each missive. He silently praised his own abilities to extract information from Trixie, then continued, "You must pardon the dramatics behind the use of the flower. The danger of my dealings requires an anonym." He laughed, enjoying the jest of how close the truth was to the lie. "We Royalists have an appreciation for the uncommon, the somewhat ridiculous. And being known as the Tulip is a foolish vanity of mine."

She gave him a considering look, then asked, "Besides your written directives, was there anything else in the pouch?"

"Ah, you quiz me still. There were, of course, the letters I received recently from London. But you must be thinking of the map. The one with the small flowers on it, showing the locations in which I will place my agents. It was the only item not sealed." He did not understand the sudden look of embarrassment that seized her.

"Unfortunately, sir, that is no longer true. I opened one of the sealed missives when I tried to discover the owner's identity."

The muscles in his cheeks twitched as he suppressed a show of victory. For he knew by her admission that he had convinced her that the pouch was his. "That is to be forgiven. It is quite natural for a lady to seek information in such a manner."

Julia stared him down. Quite natural indeed! She found that upon greater acquaintance with this man, she liked him less and less, if at all.

He watched her, puzzled by her reaction to his words. With a slight shrug, he passed on to matters of greater import. "*Mademoiselle*, I must have the pouch. Will you give it to me?"

Her countenance reflected her undecided state of mind. Everything he told her about the pouch and the papers was correct and surely only the owner would know such information. Then why did she doubt him?

"I shall need time to retrieve it," she said finally, glancing up at the house. "It is hidden."

"I will wait here while you fetch it." His sense of urgency drove him to pushing her to the point.

"No. I cannot do that." She thought of Thomas and the rector up in the Red Rooms—in the dressing-room, no doubt, right by the clothes-press. How could she get it? "I shall have to give the pouch to you later, after the fête. Perhaps tomorrow, in the late afternoon, while everyone rests from the rigours of the festival."

Philippe thought for a moment. "Do you know the place they call Wookey Hole? Meet me in the first cavern at sunset tomorrow."

"Wookey Hole? At sunset? The gate will be locked."

"It will be unlocked when you come to meet me." Seeing her raised eyebrows, he explained, "We must take care, even now. Secrecy is of the utmost importance. You must tell no one of this meeting, not even our friend the major." Philippe had seen and heard everything until Rossiter—rot his eyes—had come along and whisked her away.

"You know Major Druce?"

He smiled at her in a tolerant way. "It is my business to know things. Not knowing could end my life before I have reached my goal."

"Why have you not contacted Major Druce? The missive said you would be dealing with him."

"The major, he is too occupied with his *amour*. A man in love is dangerous. He thinks not with his head, but is ruled by his heart. I must take care, using only those who will not fail me. I know my safety will not be imperilled by one so good as you."

"Then you had better leave now, before my escort returns."

"Ah, *mademoiselle*, you have a concern for me. This is good. We will deal well together, you and I. Until sunset." He bowed, and faded into the darkness.

For no reason that Julia could think of, she began to tremble. A sound of furtive approach, though, kept her on her guard. Emerging from behind a sculptured hedge, Sarah moved toward her.

"Who was that man?" The girl's voice shook. "Was it the man with the ferret face?"

"The what?" Julia stared at her younger sister. "Whatever is the matter, Sarah? You look frightened to death."

Sarah glanced around. "Come up to our room," she whispered. "We cannot talk here."

"But I am to meet Lord Rossiter."

"Oh, him! Julia, this is important. Come, please?"

Once in their room, Sarah locked the door, sagging back against it. "I am being watched," she said in a hushed voice. "I don't know what to do. If I say anything he may kill Bounder."

"Who would want to kill Bounder?"

"Bateman, the man with the ferret face." She pulled Julia further into the room, away from the door. Then she looked about to be sure they were absolutely alone. "I shall have to blow the gaff, I suppose."

"Yes, tell me everything." Julia eased her sister down beside her on the bed and wrapped a comforting arm about the girl's waist.

Sarah drew a deep breath and recounted what had happened at the ruins on the Tor. Then she sat silent for a time. "After I got away, I thought perhaps someone was playing a trick. I kept watch to see if anyone were watching me and I never saw a soul. But tonight when I spied that man with you, I decided to play least-in-sight. What did he say? What did he look like?"

"I could not see his face, but I doubt that he was the man from the ruin." Julia spoke warily, for she wanted to keep Sarah from further misadventures. "The man who spoke to me was more cultured than you intimated about that man Bateman. I daresay someone has tried to hand you moonshine with this talk of pouches and cutting throats." She gave Sarah a consoling hug. "But to ease your mind, I shall keep Bounder close to me during the next few days. I'll let no harm come to him."

"Would you do that? You're the best of sisters. 'Tis a deuce of a job watching over everyone." Sarah got up and moved to the window. "I shall not be easy for a while yet, no matter what you say about moonshine." She gasped in surprise and pressed her nose to the pane. "Julia! Come quick! There's Harry and . . . Marion! He is kissing her."

Her eyes widened as the kiss grew deeper. "Shocking what two people in love will do."

"Come away from the window." Julia managed to turn Sarah's shoulders round. Still craning her neck, the girl gaped at the couple below. Putting a hand over Sarah's eyes, Julia led her away.

"How am I to learn anything if I am always denied knowledge of everything?" Sarah huffed. "I daresay I shall be reduced to watching the maid and groom buss and cuddle."

Julia glanced up at the ceiling and implored, "Deliver me from this brazen babe of Beelzebub."

"You sound just like Mr. Oglesby."

Julia's aghast expression froze on her face. Then she clapped a hand to her forehead and muttered, "I need a tonic. The strain is beginning to show."

"It's bound to. Mr. Oglesby is contagious. Soon you'll be spouting moral platitudes just like him." Sarah shook her head sadly. "Just imagine a whole lifetime with the man."

Julia groaned. "Please, no more. I daresay I shall have nightmares aplenty without your help. Besides, you were to be in bed long ago."

"Oh, very well, but first we *must* do something," Sarah went over to her dressing table and fetched a black velvet pincushion. "Give me the stocking from your right foot," she ordered. She took Julia's stocking and dropped the cushion full of pins in it. Then she hung the stocking at the head of Julia's bed. "There, now you shall dream of your future mate. Good night!" Looking quite pleased with herself, Sarah went to bed.

Julia, quite exhausted, slowly undressed and climbed into bed. As she pulled the coverlet up to her chin, she gazed at the charm fastened above her bed. Would she dream of her

future mate? Would it be Thomas? She shook her head. It
was utter nonsense. She closed her eyes and resolved to turn
her mind in another direction.

She wondered why there seemed all at once to be so many
people wanting the pouch. Should she give it to the man
Philippe? If so, how the devil was she to get the thing? She
fell asleep scheming. That night, as so many nights before,
her dreams were of a man with a silver patch.

SURELY PROVIDENCE had taken a hand in her life, Julia
mused as she ambled along the secluded footpath to
Wookey Hole. She held tightly to the leash in her hand,
preventing the sniffing mastiff from straying too far from
her side. Since the moment she'd excused herself after dinner, events had fallen into place as if guided by a benevo-
lent but invisible hand. After dismissing Betty for the
evening, Julia had gone to the Red Rooms. She had
thought that she would encounter Rossiter's valet, yet the
man was not in the dressing-room. Fetching the pouch was
surprisingly simple. She wondered why she'd had such
trouble before.

Getting out of the house unseen, and with Bounder in
tow, had been like a magical sleight-of-hand. She was there
one moment and gone the next, with no one the wiser. It
was remarkable.

Now, as she walked along the wooded path, a black lantern slung over her arm and cloaked in a mantle with the
pouch clutched close to her side, she had time to think
about her good fortune. It was so strange. If she were not
aware that she had acted on the impulse of the moment, she
would have sworn that it had all been planned.

The first signs of sunset began to show in the sky as she
paused to think. Bounder, though, seemed dissatisfied with
idleness and tugged to go forward. Julia stirred herself and

sighed. "I daresay we should make haste, Bounder, else we shall be late." Together they made their way through the wooded pastureland.

She hurried to the entrance of the cave, the rumbling sound of the River Axe growing louder as she neared it. At the door, which was usually locked, she paused and found it ajar. She slipped inside with Bounder leading the way. Stopping him with a strong tug, she bent to bring up the flame in her lantern. She wound the leash about her hand to pull Bounder closer to her, then ventured down the passage and the steps known as Hell's Ladder to the first cavern. Of the caverns accessible to visitors, it was the largest, measuring more than one hundred feet across. Seen from the small circle of light cast by the lantern, the cave seemed to go on forever.

Julia moved the lantern in a sweeping motion as she inched deeper into the cavern. She gasped when the light fell upon the giant stalagmite known as the Witch of Wookey, a woman alleged to have been turned to stone when a monk tried to exorcise her demons.

Everything about the cavern gave Julia a decidedly uneasy feeling—the clammy dankness, the chilling atmosphere, the reverberation of water from the River Axe. She stationed Bounder next to her as she sank to the ground and placed the lantern in front of her. Beyond the edge of the light it cast, the fingers of darkness prodded her fancy, causing all manner of nervous jumps and starts.

She determined to turn her mind away from the encroaching blackness. She laid the pouch upon her lap. Seeing it in the lamplight reminded her of the first time she had seen it. So much had happened since that night. She opened the pouch and trailed her fingers over the tulip. As she gazed at the tulip, she realized that Philippe failed to meet her imagined picture of who the Tulip should be. It was as if the man were trying to squeeze his foot into a boot not made for him. He simply did not fit.

Philippe was too coming, pushing himself upon her as the Tulip. Whoever the man behind the flower was, she felt sure he would be more subtle, with an understated finesse. Certainly he would not show the patriotism that the man Philippe had displayed to such an overt degree. Still, Philippe did know about the contents of the pouch...

Her fingers stroked the imprint of the flower. A tulip, she mused. With startling clarity, she recalled Oglesby's words—Rossiter was a tulip. Of course!

She stared at the open pouch. Could it be true? Gingerly she pulled out the unsealed missive and spread it open before her. The writing scrawled at the bottom of the list of flowers and names looked familiar. She forced her mind back to the note Harry had given her from the Tulip, then back further still to the written message Thomas's valet had delivered to her a few days before. She blinked at the firm strokes of the writing, recalling the similarities between all three of them. It was true. Thomas, Baron Rossiter of Rossiter, was the Tulip.

She sat wondering why the truth had never come to her before. Was it because she did not want to associate the identity of the Tulip with Thomas? If she had, the game would have ended. Surely there were a dozen things that should have shouted the true reason for his presence in the district—his secret meetings, his knowledge of flowers, his cryptic words to her. Yet somehow she had shut out logic. Was it his kisses that had made her mind refuse to function?

Shakily she got to her feet and tucked the pouch into the pocket of her mantle. She knew what she must do. The pouch had to be returned to its owner.

Since Rossiter was the owner, who was Philippe? A liar, no doubt. A French spy, perhaps?

The notion chilled her. And this man was imminently to meet her.

The distant sound of boot striking rock echoed through the hollow chamber. Someone was coming down Hell's Ladder.

She looked about for a place to hide, cursing her lack of a weapon. As the footsteps neared the cavern she hid under an outcrop of rock and pulled Bounder with her. After flicking shut the black lantern, she draped the full cape of her mantle over them.

"Miss Witton, are you there?"

Julia clamped a hand over Bounder's muzzle and whispered that he hush. His low growl stopped.

The light of a lantern slowly moved into the cavern. "I know you are here. I can always feel the presence of a woman. Come out, *mademoiselle*." The light swept about. "Why do you hide?"

Philippe moved around the cavern, peering into every crevice. "Charming lady, there is no need to hide. I have come to get that which is mine. Come out—now!" His voice had begun to grate. Bounder shifted in her hold, striking the darkened lantern. A stream of light flashed into Julia's eyes. She gasped.

Before she could react properly, Philippe was before her holding a pistol. She held Bounder to her side as Philippe pointed the gun at the dog's head.

"I can see by your look that I have been unmasked. I shall count to ten. If I do not have the pouch by the number ten, I shall kill the dog—first—and then . . ." He didn't

need to go on. "Do not force me to an unpleasant task."
He put his lantern down. "Hand over the pouch!"

"No."

"One. Two. Three. Four..."

CHAPTER FOURTEEN

"...Eight. Nine—"

"Stop! Please, wait!" Julia scrambled up from her crouched position, and Philippe stopped his counting. "I don't want to die!" She made crying and sniffling sounds and clutched her throat, her fingers loosening the clasp of her mantle. "You may have it." She raised the end of her voluminous cape and made as if to dry her eyes. She watched him, waiting for her chance.

He took the pocket pistol off half cock. Dispassionately, he looked at Julia as her tears built to near-hysterical sobbing, then put away his weapon. "Come, *mademoiselle*, the pouch, if you please." He held out his hand. "Enough of these vapours. Calm yourself!"

Bounder growled and bristled at Philippe's sharp tone.

Still sniffling, Julia murmured words to soothe the dog as she stroked his neck. Her mind worked rapidly, trying to figure a way out of her fix.

"The pouch, *mademoiselle*. Give it to me!"

She reached among the folds of her mantle and brought forth the leather packet. She hesitated an instant before thrusting it toward Philippe.

With a maniacal look on his face, Philippe feasted his eyes on the pouch. "I have it! Now, it shall all be mine—the lands, the title, even the renumeration from the Emperor. I have beat Rossiter!" He ran his hands over the leather again and again, chortling. Excitement seemed to build in

him as he fondled his prize. He threw back his head and
crowed in triumph.

At that moment Julia balled her hand into a fist. She
cocked her arm back and let it fly with all her might, like a
battering ram, right in the direction of Philippe's raised
chin.

They both cried out at the impact. Caught unawares in
his laughter, his jaw had snapped shut upon his tongue.
And Julia's hand stung like the devil.

Bounder rushed in to nip at Philippe's legs and heels. A
string of garbled curses came from the Frenchman as he
tried to swat the dog away and ease the pain in his tongue.
The pouch slipped from his grasp, falling near his lantern.
With a fierce, guttural roar, he charged Julia.

Philippe's onslaught was met by Bounder, who leaped
for the man's neck. Dog and man went down in a snarling
heap. The two thrashed and rolled into the encircling
darkness.

Julia snatched up her lantern and followed the sounds of
the struggle. By her lamp's light, she saw Philippe just
managing to hold off Bounder. The dog's massive teeth
were inches from the man's throat. Philippe pushed back
against the great weight that pinned him to the ground.
With one arm at Bounder's throat, Philippe worked against
the clawing paws, as he moved his hand down to the pocket
that held his gun.

Julia saw Philippe yank out the pistol. Before he could
fully cock the weapon Julia swung her lantern at his hand.
A loud report echoed through the chamber as the loose
pistol struck against the rock. The shot zipped past Julia's
ear.

Startled by the sound, Bounder raised his head from his
foe. Julia called him off Philippe, pulling on the dog's collar.

"Here, boy," she urged as she tugged. "Come, Bounder." She jerked his leash.

Collapsing back on the ground, Philippe rubbed the tattered remains of his coat sleeves. He rolled about, moaning.

Holding the resistant Bounder to her side, Julia struggled toward the pouch lying in the lamplight. She ignored Bounder's growl and pulled him on toward her goal. Too late, she felt the hand grab her ankle, and she was toppled.

Philippe wrapped his arms around her knees. She kicked him in the stomach and hammered at his head with her fists.

"It is mine!" he yelled.

"Let me go! Bounder! Get him, boy!"

The dog had been nipping at any place that did not seem to belong to his mistress. He finally sank his teeth into the leather of Philippe's boot. Growling, he pulled and tugged.

Philippe lost his hold on Julia. He snatched at her skirt as he was dragged from one end and kicked from the other.

"The pouch belongs to me," he panted. "Give it to me!"

Grabbing the edge of her mantle, Julia threw it over Philippe's head. His arms flailed wildly as he tried to free himself. She lunged for the pouch.

With Bounder still holding his leg, Philippe plunged after her and fell forward. Her lantern was just within his grasp. He threw it after her, as Bounder gave a hard tug on his leg.

The lantern went spinning crazily through the air, missing Julia, and crashed just beside the pouch. The oil spilled out, running over the pouch, and burst into flames.

Julia gasped as the small fire leaped before her. She cringed, watching the flames lick at the leather of the packet. Better no one has it, she reasoned, than that Philippe should get it.

She grabbed the other lantern as she ran for the passageway, calling for Bounder as she went. Near the entrance, she collided with someone rushing in. Her forward momentum was greater than his, and he stumbled back. She clouted him with the lantern. He tumbled to the ground, stunned. As she leaped over his inert body, she glanced down. The man had the look of a ferret. She shuddered and hurried on.

Outside, the thundering torrent of the River Axe muted every other sound, even the pounding of her heart. Bounder leaped about her, barking his boast of victory. Julia took a quick gulp of air, grabbed the dog's leash and ran for the woods.

In the deepening twilight, she could scarcely distinguish the path winding through the trees. After a few paces, she halted. Bounder frisked about sniffing the earth. He plopped down, panting happily, and barked.

"Bounder," Julia whispered, "do be quiet." She stood trying to catch her breath. As she raised her arm to brush back her tumbled hair, a man's hand grasped her around the waist. She would have cried out, but another hand clamped over her mouth.

She wondered briefly why Bounder failed to come to her aid. She struggled against being pulled into the bushes. With all her might, she kicked at the shins behind her. Still she was held fast. Her fingers clawed at the man's face. She ceased thrashing when she touched something metallic on his face.

Turning in his hold, Julia flung her arms about his neck. "Thom—" Her cry was silenced by his lips.

His mouth roamed to her ear. "Julia, you headstrong girl, whatever am I to do with you?" he whispered. He stepped back from her, looking down at her torn, dirty gown. "What the devil! What happened in there? Are you hurt?"

She leaned her head on his shoulder and sighed. "I am unharmed." She felt herself being crushed to him as a ragged sigh escaped him.

"Harry was to be in charge of the pouch, was he not?"

She squirmed uneasily in his grasp. "Yes. And he should have the message I sent to him by now. Philippe said—"

Rossiter shook his head. "I can imagine what the swine had to say. Where is he now?"

"In the cavern."

"And the pouch? Does he have it?"

She hung her head and nodded, then she brightened. "But it's burnt."

"What!"

"Shhh—"

He turned away from her, cursing under his breath. "My dear girl, bait that is burnt will hardly attract the game one desires."

"Bait? Do not tell me...those were not the real papers!"

"I have gone to great lengths these past few days to bring Vodrey and the pouch together. I need thorough evidence to hang a thorough rogue." He hugged her to him. "You were not to have any part in it, or so I planned."

Bounder crept over and sat at Julia's feet. Rossiter's harsh tone made the dog protective of her even though he recognized the man as a friend.

Thomas's expression softened. "To keep you well out of this, I went so far as to disclose my true purpose here to Harry. We spent the afternoon arranging the plans for our trap. Unfortunately we underestimated you. Harry felt sure you would honour your promise."

"And so I would have, but Philippe said…" She cursed herself for her foolishness. Then she looked at him accusingly. "Someone ought to have told me who he was—a blasted French spy!" She turned from him. "How did you know to come here, if I ruined your plans?"

"My associate, Scully, was to follow the pouch wherever it went. When you came to the caves instead of going to Harry's—where we thought you would go—he rode back to alert me."

"Now what will you do?"

He put a finger to her lips, bidding her to be silent. Cupping his hands over his mouth, he imitated the call of a nightingale. The sound of a whippoorwill answered back.

Scully emerged from the darkness a moment later and joined them. "All quiet back here?" he asked. "Minns is watchin' the entrance to the caverns. Missoor Philippe and his man are still inside."

Watching Julia's curious examination of his comrade, Rossiter began to enjoy the situation. "Miss Witton, I don't believe you have met my friend and former sergeant-major, Scully, Laibrook Scully." He smiled as the two nodded in acknowledgement of the introduction. "Well, Scully, should we go in and drag them out?"

"That wouldn't be wise," Julia interjected. "The cavern has many hiding places. There is but one way out. They will eventually have to use it."

"She's in the right of it, sir. They don't know we're waitin' to take 'em. Let's sit it out till they come. Counting the major, it is four against two. Seems fair odds when a body hunts for weasels."

"Harry's here, in the thick of it?" Julia's voice took on a note of worry.

"Did you think I'd sit at home waiting for word from you?" Harry asked, coming up behind her. Scully moved away in the direction that Harry had come from.

She hung her head, ashamed to confront Harry when she had deceived him. "I thought I could manage alone."

"Is that why you *forgot* to send me the pouch?" Harry's displeasure carried clearly in his voice. "If your father holds me responsible for your foolishness and forbids the banns, it will be your funeral we're attending in a sennight, not your wedding."

Julia looked away from Harry. "I was a fool, as you have long held me to be. But it was entirely my fault and so I shall tell Father."

The men glanced at each other. Thomas took Julia's hand. "That won't be necessary. The bishop has been in my confidence from the first. Come, I must get you away from here." The couple moved past Harry along to the path leading through the woods. Bounder followed, sniffing at the bushes and trees. "I am afraid the dog will have to serve as your escort. I want you to return home, taking the long route, if you please, to the main road."

"But—"

"Bounder will see you home safely. Now, go!"

She stood looking at him. Her eyes implored a response that he was not loathe to give. He took her in his arms and kissed her to breathlessness.

As he set her away from him, he said, "That should give you something to think about on the way home. Now, off you go." He turned her in the right direction and nudged her forward.

With steps that scarcely touched the ground, she made her way through the woods, moving past the paper mill toward the main road that led back into Wells. Her mind was filled with thoughts of Thomas. Had it not been for

Bounder, she would have wandered about all night in her dreamy daze. But he herded her along as if she were a stray lamb.

They had gone about half a mile from Wookey Hole when Bounder stopped short. He growled. Then, with head lowered, he moved cautiously forward, leaving her behind.

"Bounder," Julia softly called after him. "What is it? Here, boy."

Bounder's fierce barking came from out of the darkness, followed by a piercing scream. "Zee wolf!" A young woman ran toward Julia. "Flee! Zee wolf, he is after me."

Julia caught the young woman by the shoulder. "Wolves? Here? Nonsense!" The mastiff came leaping up, frightening the woman as he frisked about them. "Bounder, do behave. This is most unseemly."

The young woman stared at Bounder. "*Un chien!* He is a dog!" She pulled her shawl around her shoulders. "I was so terrified." She looked up at Julia. "You must help. *Madam*, she is back there still."

"*Madam?*"

"Madam Fitzsimmons. I am her maid, Marie. She is being held prisoner."

"Fitzsimmons? Lord Rossiter's stepsister?"

"*Oui!* Come, you must help me."

Julia kept the girl from rushing off. She looked back in the direction of Wookey Hole. Should she go for Rossiter?

"Hurry! There is no time to stop. That one, Philippe, he will return."

"I think not. Lord Rossiter probably has him bound and gagged by now."

"His lordship, he is here? He has captured that one?"

"Of course." Julia hoped her confidence did not exceed the deed. "Tell me, where is your mistress being held? Is it very far from here?"

Marie looked about in a confused manner. "I do not know." She peered into the dark, not sure from which direction she had come.

"What can you tell me about the place where you were held?"

The maid wrinkled her nose in distaste. "It is very old and very dirty, and it has a taproom. The kind Stokes says it was once an inn. The road to it is full of ruts and weeds. I could not find my way back there."

For a moment Julia stood thinking. "An old inn, you say?" She reviewed the possibilities and arrived at one conclusion. "Meeker's Folly. It must be the Folly. It was abandoned years and years ago." She took Marie's hand. "Come along. Let us see what we can do for your mistress."

With a countrywoman's instinct for direction, Julia led the way to the vale where the inn stood, tucked away from the eye of the casual passer-by. The overgrown track leading into the vale had been trampled from recent use, but in the darkness, the lane would have gone unnoticed by anyone not familiar with the area.

As the two women walked cautiously along the lane, accompanied by Bounder, they made plans for the rescue. Julia asked questions about how the inn was guarded and where Mrs. Fitzsimmons's room was located. Marie willingly provided the answers until Julia asked about Stokes, the one guarding the hostage.

"Please, *mademoiselle*, Abel, that is Mr. Stokes, he helped me to get away."

"Why did he do that?"

Marie stopped walking. She pulled her shawl closer about her shoulders. "He feared Philippe would harm me...and *madam*, once he had the pouch. When someone ceases to be useful to that one it is *fini*." She shrugged. "Stokes, he is good in his heart. He would not hurt us."

"We shall see. Stokes is, after all, in the pay of Philippe." She looked at the maid's worried face. "Our first concern must be for your mistress."

"But how can a woman overpower a big, strong man?"

"By using her wits. Now, come."

When they reached the edge of the inn yard, Julia stopped and crouched behind the stone wall that surrounded the grounds. "We'll enter through the back, by the kitchen." She took Bounder's leash from her hand and gave it to Marie. "I am putting you in charge of him. Keep him quiet and follow me."

A gentle night breeze ruffled Julia's hair as she led the way to the back of the inn. The faint light coming from the covered windows showed the way across the yard to the rear door. Rusty hinges nearly gave their presence away as Julia eased inside. She paused with the door only half-open and held her breath, waiting for Stokes to come to investigate the noise. A full minute went by without any indication that they had been discovered.

Julia deftly manoeuvred around the half-open door, then motioned for Marie to follow. The maid entered quietly. But as Bounder came after her, his large mass filling the doorway, he pushed the small opening wider. The hinges protested with a loud squeak.

Julia and Marie stood frozen, listening. No one came.

From the floor above a voice let fly a chorus of shrieks. "Curse you, Stokes! My hair is not a horse's mane. I shall never forgive Marie for leaving me at a time like this. How she could go off before brushing my hair is beyond me. The girl has no sense of duty. She is always thinking only of herself. My hardships mean little to her. Oh, how I have suffered. Give me that brush, you heavy-handed idiot. And get out! Get out!''

CHAPTER FIFTEEN

THE STAIRS OF THE OLD INN creaked with the tromp of heavy feet after Stokes hastened from Trixie's chamber. His lumbering steps halted in the taproom. Stokes drew his third tankard of ale from the keg that rested on the bar. Raising the vessel to his lips, he drank deeply, then set the empty tankard down with a ringing clang.

"Cursed woman," he muttered, wiping his lips with the back of his hand. He stared at the flickering tallow candles in the wall bracket, his eyes suddenly seeming to see a vision that turned his plain face sad. "Marie," he said softly.

Marie cried out just as Julia let the unwieldy pan fall on the back of Stoke's head. For an instant he merely stood there, then he wavered to and fro until he fell forward with a crash.

"You have killed him!" Marie rushed toward Stokes, dragging Bounder's cumbrous weight after her by the leash. She knelt beside the fallen henchman and caressed his head, sobbing all the while into her shawl. Bounder wandered around to the man's other side and licked his ear.

From the floor above, Trixie pounded on the door of her chamber, demanding to know what was taking place. Julia shouted up to her. "Be still. Please!"

"Oh," Marie cried, "he has the bump coming up on his head." She turned angrily to Julia. "Did you have to strike him with such force?"

"But I didn't! The pan slipped. It fell more from its own weight than from my intent to hit him." Julia bent down to look at Stokes. "He still breathes. Perhaps he is just stunned."

"I pray it is so."

Again Trixie hammered on her door. "Stokes! Stokes, you freak of nature, answer me! Who is down there with you? Stokes? Stokes!"

"Come," Julia said, placing her hand under Marie's arm, "your mistress needs you. She sounds...overset."

Marie slowly got to her feet. "*Bien sur*, I must go to *madam*." But she stayed looking at Stokes. Then, with a noisy sob, she turned and ran out of the taproom door.

"Bounder, stay," Julia ordered. "Guard him." Bounder circled Stokes, then plopped down on top of him, his great weight pinning the man to the floor.

Julia left the taproom and entered the receiving hall at the front of the inn. A single lamp lit the area, keeping the outer door in the shadows.

As Julia began to mount the stairs, she heard Trixie's reproachful voice. "So, Marie, there you are. You have come to your senses, have you? I shall not reproach you. But how you could go off without a thought about me...?" She sniffed. "How unspeakably loathsome for you to be out dallying with that dunderhead, Stokes. Well, you may brush my hair. I have been sorely neglected of late."

Taking a deep breath, Julia proceeded up the remaining steps. At the top of the stairs she came to a small landing that allowed access to the guest chambers. Julia wrinkled her nose. The smell of rotting timber permeated the air of the landing, and yellow water marks streaked the walls. This atmosphere of disuse stayed with Julia until she crossed over the open threshold of Trixie's room.

The odour of stale perfume pervaded it, as if its occupant had doused everything with scent. The boarded-over windows could give scant relief from the acrid smell. The Spartan furnishings—a sagging bed, a broken wash-stand, and an oddly leaning chair—clashed with the dainty elegance of the lady, who somehow found a way to drape herself gracefully in the chair.

"Lud, how many women does that lout, Stokes, need?" Trixie turned to Marie. "Just look at her hair and gown." She shuddered as she gazed disdainfully at Julia.

Drawing herself up to her full height, Julia said, "I am Miss Julia Witton, Mrs. Fitzsimmons. We have met on several occasions during the Season in Town. I am not surprised that you fail to recognize me, as you so seldom take notice of members of your own sex." She quietly regarded Trixie for a moment. "Your maid and I have come to help you. If you would dress, we will leave this place. You must be weary of staying here."

Trixie eyed Julia contemptuously. "Who did you say you were?" She waved her hand in a dismissive manner. "Oh, it does not signify. You are correct, I *am* weary of this horrid place. I have not been treated well at all. Philippe was cruel to me. Look at my hair!" She tossed a dull, limp curl over her shoulder. "I was forced to use soap not fit for a farmer's wife. I have never known such cruelty." She cast Julia a soulful expression and dabbed at a tear, as if she were practicing for some future performance.

"I am sure you have experienced, ah, the most unspeakable of horrors." Julia found herself holding back a smile when she spied a container of bonbons sitting on the bed.

"I have!" Trixie nodded emphatically. "And so I shall tell my husband, Fitz. He would not dare to scold me when he hears all that I have had to endure." She began to cry in her pretty way. "It was simply horrible."

Julia softly cleared her throat. "After your maid has helped you dress, you shall feel more the thing, and then we can leave."

"Marie!" Trixie shut off her tears as she sharply called for her maid's attention. "You may dress my hair, then begin to pack my things while I choose what I shall wear."

Marie looked from her mistress to Julia.

"Perhaps you failed to understand, ma'am," Julia said slowly, holding tight to her patience. "We have come to rescue you. We must leave at once, as soon as you dress."

"I will not leave without my things." Trixie rose to face Julia, who dominated the petite woman by a good eight inches. But the superior look on Trixie's face clearly indicated she intended to get her way. "Pack my things, Marie," she ordered, her gaze still fixed on Julia. The maid waited to hear what Julia would say.

A strong desire to throttle Mrs. Fitzsimmons took possession of Julia. For Thomas's sake she fought the impulse. It was for him that she had come to this forgotten place, and for him she would tolerate this peevish beauty.

"Pack quickly, Marie," Julia ordered. "But as for dressing your hair, *madam*, you may tuck it under a cap, or some such thing. We leave in twenty minutes—dressed or not, packed or not."

Trixie bristled, turning a haughty shoulder to Julia. "Marie, fetch my trunk!"

"Trunk?" Julia watched Trixie flounce past her into the next room. "Surely she does not mean to take a trunk?"

Marie nodded in a resigned fashion as she followed her mistress. The maid reached the doorway and looked back. "*Madam*, she is so stupid," she whispered.

AT WOOKEY HOLE, Philippe stood just inside the entrance holding the scorched remains of the pouch. With the aid of

Julia's mantle he had quelled the fire before it had done much damage to the papers inside. Then he had made his way out, and he now held those missives as if he held the deed and title to all the world.

Bateman, the one Julia had struck with the lantern, crawled over to Philippe and pulled himself up to lean dazedly against the wall. "Are you goin' after her?"

A look of molten hatred spoiled Philippe's perfect face. His hand curled around the edges of the papers until he clutched them in a fierce grip. A bit of charred paper fell off into his hand and he watched as the browned fragments fluttered to the ground. A deep guttural sound came from between his pressed lips.

"She will be taken care of, never fear." Philippe's eyes narrowed. "A woman has yet to deal me a trick which she has not lived to regret . . . for the rest of her life."

His tone made even his cruel henchman shiver.

Turning from the opening of the cave, Philippe went back along the tunnel until his foot struck the lantern that Julia had discarded. The impact with Bateman's head had left the lantern only slightly damaged, and it was still serviceable. Philippe bent over and worked until the wick caught flame. He carried the light to where Bateman leaned against the wall.

Both men looked as if they had tangled with a wild vixen and lost. Philippe tore the shredded remains of his neckcloth from about his throat. The heir to the Vodrey title had come close to losing his life.

"Make ready. We leave after I have rested," Philippe said, giving his flunky's battered condition no thought. "Did you secure the horses in a place nearby?"

"Aye, they be tethered behind the mill, away from the main path. Seems too quiet out there," Bateman said, looking out at the darkening landscape.

Philippe glanced disdainfully at him. "That wench has knocked your courage loose. Your mind is imagining spooks where there are none." He took the lantern to the other side of the passage and settled against the wall. Reverently he eased the papers back into the pouch and tucked it into a hidden pocket inside his coat. Then he sank to the ground and raised his knees to prop his arms on. Tired from his struggle with Bounder and Julia, he leaned his head on his arms and rested.

A short time later, Philippe felt a hand upon his shoulder. "Never touch me," he uttered without lifting his head. He drew breath slowly. "What is it, Bateman?"

"I saw somebody movin' out there."

Philippe glanced at the entrance, then back at his man. "It is time to leave."

"But I tell you—" Bateman's words were choked off by the Frenchman's hand.

"And I tell you, we are leaving. Now, give me your pistol." With one hand on the man's throat, Philippe held out his other for the gun. His fingers tightened, closing off Bateman's air, until the fellow complied. "You are wiser than I thought. We shall see just how wise you are. You must follow my instructions. You can take orders, can't you?" Philippe waved the pistol under the man's nose.

Bateman nodded, wondering what Philippe would have him do. His face twitched nervously.

"Stop shaking, coward! You'll not die yet. Men like you live far too long. Now, this is what you are to do..." Philippe went on to sketch his plans and give Bateman his part in them.

"I'll wager there is a whole squadron of men out there," whined Bateman. "I swear I saw a uniform. Militia, mayhap?"

"Imbecile, if that band of local blunderers were out there, they'd have raised such a racket you would not be left to wonder." Philippe pulled his coat around his neck, hiding his white shirt. He rubbed dirt on his face and hands, and made his henchman do likewise. "Keep low and keep moving."

At Philippe's signal, Bateman crept out of the cave. He quickly disappeared into the woods without giving rise to an outcry of discovery.

Grabbing up the remains of Julia's mantle, Philippe dropped it in a heap at the mouth of the cave. He used his coat to shield the light, then, just as he slipped away, he threw the lantern onto the mantle.

Minns and Scully motioned to each other when flames burst out at the entrance of the cave. They cautiously hurried forward to investigate. Quickly looking around, Scully whistled a signal to alert Rossiter that Philippe had taken French leave.

"Best get over to the major," Scully whispered to Minns. "He's watchin' their horses."

So intent was he upon watching the horses, in fact, that Harry failed to hear the stealthy approach from behind. He turned only in time to receive a pistol butt on the side of his head. He dropped to the ground, aware of nothing other than a shooting pain, then blackness.

Pocketing the pistol, Philippe joined Bateman by the horses. "They're all around us. Quick, man!"

Bateman leaped into the saddle and brought his rearing horse under control. From behind, Philippe whacked the gelding's haunches with a branch and shouted, sending the mount charging in the direction of Minns and Scully.

In a flash Philippe was in his own saddle, galloping in the opposite direction. Hurdling fallen logs, weaving through the trees, he made his way with all possible speed out of the woods. He heard shouts behind him and the crack of a pistol firing, but he never pulled up, not even when the ball penetrated his leg above the knee.

"Curse these English," he muttered to the wind.

"CURSE THESE ENGLISH," Marie said under her breath as she lifted her end of the heavy trunk.

"I see no reason for this unseemly haste," Trixie said with a pout.

Julia bit her lip to hold back the words that pressed to get out. She took a steadying breath. "Stokes was unconscious when I left him, with Bounder standing guard, but I cannot be certain how long he will stay that way. Mrs. Fitzsimmons, if you would take the bandboxes—"

"What!" Trixie's eyes flashed. "You want *me* to carry those heavy things? Do you take me for a lackey?" She tossed back her head angrily, offended that anyone dared tell *her* to do anything.

"Your maid and I shall have quite enough to do handling this trunk. We will not take the bandboxes too."

"Well!" Trixie pulled out her fan and waved it briskly before her face. "I can see that you are a callous female with no compassion for the hardship of others. After all I have suffered, to expect me to carry my own—"

"Take them or leave them!" Julia shifted her grip on the trunk. "You choose. But make haste!"

Grabbing two bandboxes, Trixie went before the pair who bore her travelling chest. She complained every step of the way down the stairs.

"Shh!" Marie adjured. She cocked her head to the side, straining to hear, then looked at Julia. "Did you hear it?"

Julia set her end of the trunk down at the foot of the stairs. She experienced a prickly feeling at the back of her neck.

The front door was thrown open, slamming against the wall. A dark form filled the entry.

Trixie gasped and dropped the bandboxes. The contents of one spilled out onto the floor. "Philippe!" She staggered back at the sight of him. His dirty face, tattered clothes, and blood-soaked breeches made him hardly recognizable. But the look of red-hot anger on his face was something that Trixie had seen before.

Philippe surveyed the three women in front of him. His nostrils flared. He drew the pistol and waved it from one to the other. "Trixie, *mon amour*, are you leaving? Have I been a miserable host to you?"

"I...I..." Trixie swallowed quickly. "It was not my idea to leave! This very rude woman ordered me to go with her. I had no choice in the matter. Philippe, my darling, you know that I would never leave you." Fearful of the look in his eyes, she stepped back.

He bowed in a mocking way to Julia. "Ah, the very busy Miss Witton. There is no end to your meddling, is there?" Then he noticed how much closer she was to the taproom door than when he had first come in. "Stay where you are! Do not provoke me too far. Even now I would gladly put a hole through your cunning heart." He aimed the gun at her chest.

Julia regarded him silently. He looked murderous. Then she said, "You are a bit out of sorts, sir. No doubt due to the wound to your leg. I doubt that you and Rossiter have been exchanging civilities. Is he well?"

Philippe snorted. "He has the devil's own luck. It has to be luck that aided him in that shot from such a distance. No man is that good with a pistol." He looked down at his leg and swayed slightly. "Trixie, my sweet angel, come here and bind my wound. I bleed like a stuck pig." He smiled at her, as if all were forgiven.

Called upon to look at the blood that oozed from the small hole, Trixie shrank back and shuddered. "I cannot!"

"Do not be foolish!" Philippe took a halting step toward her. "Come here, angel. You would not want me to faint from the loss of blood."

"Marie," Trixie called in a fading voice. "Come, help me attend to his injured limb." She shoved the girl toward Philippe.

Marie fell sprawling at his feet. She pulled herself up, then looked at the wound. "I need some bits of cloth."

"Trixie, get them," he ordered.

Dumbfounded, Trixie looked helplessly about. "Where do I get bits of cloth?"

"Use one of your petticoats from that bandbox," Julia suggested, pointing to the spilled articles of clothing on the floor.

"But they are new from the modiste," Trixie objected.

"Use them!" Philippe waved the pistol toward the petticoats.

"Oh, very well." Trixie sniffed tearfully as she tried to rip the fine linen into strips. She was utterly inept at the task.

"Here," Julia said, coming forward, "let me do that." She took the petticoat from Trixie and pushed her away from Philippe. After constructing a makeshift bandage, Julia passed it to the maid, then stepped back to watch Marie tie the cloth around the Frenchman's thigh.

When she had finished, Marie stepped away and moved to stand before the door to the taproom.

Philippe waved his pistol, motioning for them to group together. He dragged himself to the stairs and let out a ragged breath as he eased himself down on the trunk.

"Where is Stokes?" he asked.

"The *mademoiselle*, she knocked his head with a large pan," Marie swallowed, pushing back her rising tears. "He is still without the senses."

A hard laugh burst from Philippe as he moved his gaze to Julia. "You appear to have your hand in everything. You must learn not to be quite so busy. I see I must teach you a lesson." An evil smile spread across his lips. "Some might say that my way of instruction is harsh, but it is most effective."

"I need no tutelage from you, sir." Julia raised her chin, scornful of any threat he might deliver.

Philippe levelled his pistol at Marie. "Unless you obey me, the wench dies. Get me something to drink."

Julia regarded him for a moment, then went into the taproom and came back with a full tankard of ale. She thrust it into his hand and stepped away.

He downed the ale without pausing for breath. Smirking, he tossed the tankard back to Julia. "If you were not such a treacherous lady, Miss Witton, I would be tempted to take you with me." He grabbed Trixie by the arm. "My devoted one, you shall have the honour of coming with me."

"What?" Trixie's eyes widened in dismay.

He sneered at her. "Of the lot, my sweet, you are the least likely to stab me in the back the moment I turn around. And the companionship of a woman will make the journey and the crossing much more enjoyable. Besides, I shall need someone to tend the wound after I find a doctor to remove the shot." He gave a mirthless laugh. "I would not deny you the pleasure of my company." He nudged her toward the open door with the tip of the pistol.

Perhaps it was more Trixie's pitiful look than the desire to foil Philippe and his plan that set Julia in motion. "Philippe," she shouted as, dragging his wounded leg, he pushed Trixie before him and sidled through the door. He looked back. Julia grabbed one of Trixie's petticoats and tossed it at his head, then slammed the tankard against his injured leg. He howled and fell in the doorway.

"Run!" Julia yelled at Trixie.

For once, Trixie obeyed her and fled into the darkness. Marie darted into the taproom and slammed the door behind her. As Julia turned to follow the maid, her gown was caught and she was pulled down beside Philippe. His hand grasped her throat as his gun pressed into her ribs.

"By the saints, you shall pay for this, you meddlesome old maid!" His eyes seemed to burn away her gown. "You are a maiden, still. Pure, untouched. But not for long. When I've finished with you, not even the scarred Tulip will want you." He ran his fingers down her neck.

She glared at him coldly. "Beware, sir. There'll be the devil to pay if you ravish the daughter of a bishop. You will rot in hell!"

"*Mon dieu*, but you have spirit. Breaking you shall give me much pleasure."

"Swine!"

He tightened his hand about her throat. "Take care, chaste lady." He took his hand from her neck and slid it down her arm. "Now, help me up." When she failed to obey him, he jabbed the pistol into her side.

As she pulled him to his feet, she heard hoofbeats approaching. Julia tried to push past Philippe to the outside, but he held her to him.

"Do not call out, or you shall die," he whispered as he awkwardly yanked her back into the entrance hall. With his arms about her, he put the pistol on full cock. When she began to squirm he struck her on the side of the head. She sagged in his arms, which nearly sent him tumbling back. But Philippe held her up at the cost of great pain to his leg.

In a moment Rossiter entered, breathing heavily and holding a pistol of his own. He looked at the odd way Julia leaned in Philippe's arms. "What have you done to her?" he demanded.

"I am teaching her to be docile, something you have failed to do." Philippe caressed Julia's cheek with his gun.

"If you have—"

"That comes later." The look that Rossiter gave him quite satisfied Philippe's tormenting nature.

Julia moaned and opened her eyes. "Thomas?"

"Sorry for the delay in arriving, my dear," he said, smiling at her in a reassuring way. "But 'twas devilish hard finding the place. If you would just step away from Vodrey there, I'll relieve you of his company."

Philippe tightened his grip on Julia and held her before him like a shield. "I think not, Rossiter. I find I greatly desire the companionship of this woman. She is coming with me to France. A man of your interests should understand my wish to explore the delicate petals of this bud of delight." The pleasure he experienced as he saw Rossiter's reaction to his words was much better than that he found in laying with a woman. "She will probably kick and thrash about, even scream and bite, but we both know that in her heart she will enjoy every moment of her surrender to me." As if his taunts were not enough, he raised his hand from her waist and inched upward to her breast, daring Rossiter to charge him. One shot and it would be *fini*.

CHAPTER SIXTEEN

THE LAMPLIGHT FLICKERED on Rossiter's face, emblazing the silver patch. He struggled to control the emotions which raged within him at the sight of Vodrey fondling Julia. Though he knew that Philippe was goading him, Thomas found it impossible to stand by and do nothing. He advanced a few steps farther into the room, saying, "I won't let him harm you, my dear. Think of him as a bothersome pest you'll soon be rid of."

Philippe jeered. "You know you cannot stop me, Tulip. I might hurt the lady if you tried. You would never risk that." He ran the tip of his pistol down Julia's cleavage and then back up again. "I've the upper hand and you know it."

Julia went rigid at the insults Philippe was dealing to her body. She vowed that, come what may, the man would pay for his outrages. When she flinched from his touch, he merely laughed.

"There, there, *ma belle*," Philippe said, his lips near her ear, "you shall see how well we get along. Think of it. Rossiter, there, can think of little else. The thoughts of it are driving him to madness. See how his eye burns with it." He sniggered. "Lord Rossiter, confess, you cannot stop me. I have the lady and the papers." He saw Rossiter's look of surprise. "Yes, I have the pouch and your missives... and the map showing where your spies work. The paper is a bit charred, but still intact. It must vex you to know that I have succeeded, and you have failed. I have it all, and you have nothing. Ah, life is good!"

"I daresay," Rossiter drawled, "that you think to get a reward for your deeds of daring." He chuckled. "I wonder how surprised the Little General will be when he discovers he's been duped with sham papers and a list of fictitious names. He will undoubtedly reward you with the favours of Madam Guillotine."

Philippe's face whitened. "Liar! You would say anything to save the girl and the papers. Anything! You are jealous of me. The English have always been jealous of the French. I have what you want, what you'll die trying to get." He moved the barrel of the gun from beneath Julia's breasts. "I have prolonged your existence for too long, Monsieur Tulip." He levelled his pistol at Rossiter and placed his finger over the trigger.

Julia brought her freed arm up, catching Philippe unaware, and flung his hand upward as the pistol fired. They struggled, one working to get free, the other holding on.

Try as he might, Thomas could not get a clear shot at Philippe. He started to rush forward, but stopped.

Vodrey grunted and went curiously still. Then he staggered forward, sending both he and Julia toppling to the floor. Moaning, he tried to reach behind him and pull the knife from his back. Then he collapsed.

In the doorway of the taproom stood Scully. He shrugged at Rossiter's surprised look, as if dismissing his unhandsome but necessary act.

Thomas moved Philippe off of Julia, then lifted her up into his arms and carried her over to the trunk. "Are you hurt?"

She shook her head. Her gaze was drawn to Philippe and the knife. "Is he dead?"

Moving to block her view of the grisly scene, Thomas eased her back against the newel post. "Rest here while I see to him." He went to kneel beside Philippe. The signs of a life quickly slipping away were upon the Frenchman's face.

Philippe opened his haze-clouded eyes. He stared at Thomas. Shifting his hand, Philippe clutched his coat, beneath which lay the packet. "The papers were genuine, weren't they?" he asked in a faint voice.

Thomas shook his head slowly.

"*Alors,* you win, Tulip." Vodrey sighed deeply, letting go of his tenuous hold on life.

JULIA HUDDLED in Rossiter's greatcoat, as she stood by the horses in the yard of the inn. The man himself was still within. Harry led Bounder up to her, saying, "I found him tied to a post out back." He looked down at the mastiff. "Smells like he's lapped a goodly portion of ale." Bounder stumbled and fell at Julia's feet, giving evidence to Harry's surmise.

"Marie must have given the stuff to poor Bounder so she could help Stokes get away," Julia said, looking at the sorry state of the dog. "Have you found the two of them yet?" She wanted to keep from thinking about the subject most on her mind—the man who lay dead in the entry hall.

"Not a sign of 'em for miles around."

Julia was not surprised that Marie had run off with Stokes. She could not help smiling as she wondered what Trixie would do without the maid to wait on her. "Will Mrs. Fitzsimmons be staying with us at the manor?" A note of dread crept into her voice.

"You needn't concern yourself with the prospect of having the lady as a guest. Rossiter is seeing to her now. I believe he is bundling her off to her husband post-haste."

Harry chuckled. "Never met a woman so prone to tears, yet somehow she manages not to shed a single drop. Most interesting, how her eyes just sort of shimmer." He laughed as he adjusted the bandage around his head. "She swears she won't go anywhere until someone dresses her hair and she has her trunk and boxes. She is probably still fuming in Rossiter's chaise."

Pulling the greatcoat tighter about her shoulders, Julia turned and walked a little away. "He is not like his sister, is he?"

Harry watched her for a moment before answering. "Are you speaking of Rossiter? He is merely her stepbrother. Bound to make a difference, what with different bloodlines and all. Though they are both a bit particular about their dress, but these similar penchants can be explained. After it all, Rossiter's not a bad fellow, once one knows him better."

"Once one knows... Harry, are you roasting me? Why, anyone with a little perception can see that the man is an out and outer in all situations."

"I'll be sure to pass that sterling testimonial on to Faith when next I see her. It is sure to raise her opinion of Lord Rossiter. For she is the only one left. Sarah's too young, Marion's mine, and *you* are about to marry."

"Oh, do stop ragging me about Oglesby and this wedding. It is neither here nor there, truly."

Harry raised his brows dubiously. "Neither here nor there, hey? Tell that to Oglesby when he's standing at the altar in seven days' time. Seven days!"

She glared at him. "I can count. I know when the blasted thing is to be."

He stepped back and frowned at her. "Julia, be sensible. There will be the devil to pay if you allow this travesty to go on."

"What is the point of calling it off if..." She looked down. "If I have no better offer, if no one else wants to wed me?"

Harry stared at her. "Are you mad?" The major would have said more, but he would not take up another man's wooing. "A gentleman can hardly be expected to speak when the lady is promised to another."

"My betrothal did not stop *you* from offering, in a manner of speaking, to take me north to Gretna Green."

"Will you have done with reminding me of my near-fatal mistake? Not for the world and all its gold would I carry you to the border."

"As if I would ask such a thing when you and Marion are practically betrothed."

"Banns will be read Sunday. The bishop was to announce it to the family this evening."

At this news she threw her arms about him and embraced him with good cheer. She leaned back and regarded him, a teasing light in her eyes. "You are a marvellous campaigner, Harry. Quick to the field, quick into action and quick to victory. Simply marvellous!"

"Marvellous, hey? But not fascinating like some fellows I could name," he returned with a twinkle. "Have done with Oglesby, and take Rossiter in his stead. After all, what would you be relinquishing—a stiff-necked parson?"

The corners of her mouth turned up as she gazed into the darkness. Her expression became dreamy as she thought of all that she might have by casting off Oglesby. Thomas was intriguing, never stodgy. He was so alive, and the rector was so stagnant.

She sighed. Even if she could cast aside her obligation to honour, dare she go to her father and ask to be released from her pledge to Oglesby when she was still unsure of Thomas's intentions? Polite society would condemn her if she withdrew from the suit without sufficient reason. She wondered at the calm she felt when faced with such a prospect.

Her reverie was broken when Scully came tromping out the front door of the inn, a long, heavy bundle slung over his shoulder. The form of a man wrapped in a blanket was unmistakable. She turned away at the sight of a pair of boots protruding from the rolled-up blanket as Scully tossed it over the back of Vodrey's horse.

Harry took his leave of Julia by saying, "I'm to help the fellow take the Frenchman's body to the Black Wood. It will appear as if Vodrey met with highwaymen and perished in a struggle. Better that way. Vodrey's father is a proud nobleman who would suffer if the family name were tarnished. Besides, Rossiter wants the whole affair hushed and closed." He flicked the end of her nose and bid her adieu. Mounting his horse, he followed Scully down the track leading away from the inn.

Except for the dog who lay curled up at her feet, she stood alone in the darkness. Bounder hiccupped in his sleep. She smiled as she nuzzled the caped collar of Thomas's greatcoat. The events of the night had drained her. She felt as if she would fall asleep herself if she stood there much longer. She was scarcely aware that Rossiter had come out of the inn until he put his hands upon her shoulders and pulled her back against him.

"Your family must be wondering what's become of you. It is quite late." His voice was low and strained.

"Sarah will see that no one suspects I am other than in my bed with the headache."

For some odd reason, he smiled. "I hope you do not make a habit of having the headache when you go to bed."

His words prompted her desire to bring him to the point, ending her suspense. "Why should my habits concern you?"

"Now, there you have me. It is curious how a man can fall into being concerned for his fellows. Anything can bring on this philanthropic bent—a pesky Frenchman, a lady in distress, a pistol held to one's heart. Most curious how these odd notions come about; no accounting for them, my dear."

She turned a little and glanced up at his face. The patch winked down at her. No, she supposed it would be futile to get him to account for his feelings or their cause. Abjectly she stepped away from him.

He walked to his horse and mounted. Then he held out his hand to her. "Coming?" Thomas smiled when she hesitated. "I took the liberty of sending Trixie on with Minns, in the carriage. After your close association with her, I felt you would prefer to dispense with any further companionship." He watched her eye the cozy space that she was to occupy in front of him in the saddle. "Harry and Scully had need of the other nags. If you would rather, if it bothers your sense of propriety too much, you may ride and I'll walk." He cast his challenge with another smile.

Raising her head to look him in the eye, she placed her hand in his and jumped up. He caught hold of her and set her before him. She sat facing the side, her legs resting atop one of his in a most intimate manner. Glancing at him, she could see that he was enjoying her predicament.

"I daresay you find this situation much to your liking." She kept her gaze directed straight ahead of her, refusing to share in his amusement.

"Come now, my dear, you must admit that if the worthy Oglesby found us thus, there would be no end to his homilies. Fellow might go so far as to demand that I meet him at dawn on the field of honour. Of course, he has excused my liberties in the past, but we cannot count on his overlooking repeated offences." He set his horse in motion, pulling Julia closer to him as she slipped awkwardly at the abrupt movement. He held his mount to a walk as they made their way down the rutted lane.

"Thomas, what would happen if I severed my engagement to Mr. Oglesby?" She leaned her head upon his shoulder, hoping to make clearer the meaning of her question.

He let go of a relieved sigh. "So you have come to your senses at last."

She raised her head to look at him. "Just suppose that I came to my senses, what would happen then?"

"Hard as this may sound to you, I doubt that the rector would blow his brains out in despair. But one can always hope for such a happy outcome. His palms will likely become a sodden mess from his frustration over the cancelled honeymoon. Bound to make any man a bit out of sorts to have his pleasure denied him."

She sat rigid before him. This was hardly what she had hoped to hear. She was tired, spent by the happenings of the evening, yet her senses were alive. There were unexpressed emotions that stirred between them, she was sure of it. She merely wanted confirmation of those feelings, or a pledge from him that would put to rest all her doubts.

But the remainder of the ride to the manor house was completed in silence. Rossiter gave her no words of reassurance.

Upon reaching the gravel drive leading up to the portico, Thomas saw his carriage waiting on the main road a short distance away. He cursed softly, then let Julia down before dismounting. He took her by the arm and began to lead her up to the house when his name was called from behind a clump of bushes. Trixie stepped around the leafy branches and came toward them, pulling the hood of her travelling cloak closer to her face as she approached.

"Thomas, what is the meaning of this?" Trixie demanded. "Surely you do not intend that I travel tonight! Not after all my afflictions. That fool man of yours informed me, quite curtly, that we are going on. I refuse to go another mile until I am fit to be seen in public."

"Beatrice—"

"Thomas, do not use that hateful name. You know I loathe it."

His look became more and more intransigent with each moment he spent with his stepsister. "Very well, Mrs. Fitzsimmons—"

"You are as hateful as your father was." She sniffed and her bottom lip trembled. "Your family has never liked me. They sent me away when my mama died. They have always been cruel."

"You ran away. But that is neither here nor there. This is hardly the time to dredge up the family history." His words were barbed.

"I see that you still harbour a grudge against me for taking that pouch. You must learn to forgive others their little weaknesses. You must be more tolerant of the sensibilities of those of us with delicate natures." Trixie filled her eyes with tears. "I tell you I cannot travel without being properly dressed."

"*Madam*, since Fitz has assured me you will not be showing your face in society for a very long time, how you look is superfluous. Save for the family, no one will view your beauty for an age or more—until you have become quite forgotten by the ton." He ignored her broken sob. "Why, mayhap Fitz will now have enough of your time to produce an heir." He grimaced at her pitiful wail.

"Never! I shall never ruin my form with a child. The process is too disgusting for words."

"Tut, tut," he said with a shake of his head. "Your husband's last words to me were, 'Bring her home and I shall see she is kept too busy to think of Frenchmen. A babe a year is what she needs.'"

Trixie paled and fell back. "The monster! The fiend! What does he take me for, a sow?"

Thomas refrained from answering.

"You men are all of a breed," Trixie mumbled between sobs. "Base, vicious, rutting beasts. The woman who marries you, Thomas, would have to be insane. Only a madwoman would have you!"

He looked at Julia and murmured, "Now, what was it the moon does to you?"

Trixie stamped her foot. "Listen to me, Rossiter! I will not go."

Thomas cupped his hands and whistled toward the road. His valet came silently in answer to the summons.

"Minns, see Mrs. Fitzsimmons to the carriage," Thomas ordered.

"I won't go!" Trixie stood firmly before him with a pout on her lips.

Without looking at his stepsister, Thomas said, slowly and in a low voice bare of patience, "If she gives you an ounce of trouble, Minns, tie and gag her. That is an order."

"You wouldn't dare." Trixie's words were brave, but her voice wavered on them.

"There is nothing he wouldn't dare," Julia vouchsafed.

Trixie looked Julia up and down. "And you are just like him." She flounced off to the carriage before Minns.

"The viper," Thomas commented as he watched his stepsister climb into the chaise. "She won't be pleasant company for me."

"You are leaving for London, too?" Julia's words seemed to come from far away, carried on a whisper of air.

Thomas looked at her. "I must accompany my stepsister. Besides, surely you do not expect me to stay for your wedding to the worthy Oglesby?"

"Yes—no! That is, I thought you might want to...to put an end to it."

"But I was told not to interfere."

"When did you ever let that stop you?" Then, sick of playing with words, she blurted, "Thomas, don't you want me?"

Taking her by the hand, he pulled her down the drive, away from the carriage. He stopped abruptly and took her in his arms. He looked at her upturned face for a moment. Slowly he began to kiss her, tightening the embrace, kiss after kiss. When at last he drew his head away from hers, ending the fiery touch of their lips, he stepped back.

"If that does not put an end to this nonsense about marriage to a milksop, parish-prig...then have the glue-pot and be demned, the lot of you!" He turned to leave, but stopped. Not facing her, he said, "You are my Titania. You know that, don't you?" He did not see her nod, and he stalked off to the carriage without once looking back.

CHAPTER SEVENTEEN

JULIA RUSHED DOWN the main stairs early the next morning. Coming upon the butler in the morning-room, she said, "Cleeves, I must speak to the bishop as soon as may be. Would you relay my request for a private interview?"

The butler masked his look of curiosity. "His lordship has been called away, but should be returning within the hour. Shall I convey your wishes upon his arrival?"

"Yes, do. In the meantime, kindly tell Mr. Oglesby that I must see him in the small drawing-room in twenty minutes. Tell him the matter is urgent."

She paced away the time of her waiting, her thoughts crowding in on her. Her steps became lengthened and more rapid. Oh, why had she not ended this foolish engagement long ago? she chastised herself. Did duty and notions of the honourable thing outweigh the consideration one should give to happiness...and love? She closed her eyes as a wave of doubt washed over her. Would Thomas ask her to marry him? He seemed to view the necessity of having a wife as a caprice of society. After all, what need had he for a wife when he had a troupe of opera dancers at his beck and call?

It was true that she was his to claim if he wanted her. She loved him. She only prayed that her being his Titania meant everything to him, as it meant everything to her. Oh why, she asked herself for the thousandth time, could he not speak straightforwardly?

The opening of the drawing-room door brought her out of her thoughts. "Mr. Oglesby," she said coolly, proffering two fingers for him to grasp.

"Dear lady, when I heard of your malady last night, I was sure that your disorder of late had come back to visit you. Was it the moon again?"

"No, it was not the moon, sir. I have at last come to my senses." She faced him squarely. "We must terminate our engagement."

"Miss Witton! Do not joke. This will not do. It simply will not do." He drew a sheaf of paper out of the pocket of his frock coat. "I have given much thought to our future. I have listed a few items which I believe will allow you to conform to the comportment expected of a rector's wife." He shuffled the papers, reviewing with a fond eye his words of wisdom. "To begin with—"

"Mr. Oglesby, pray stop! It is not necessary to continue." She took a calming breath. "As much as it grieves me to say this, I feel I must. I am not worthy of the honour you would bestow if you gave your name to me. Mrs. Atley Oglesby must be a woman of unquestionably upright character, not given to fancy or odd humours. She must be all that is good." She bowed her head. "Mrs. Oglesby is a title to which I cannot aspire. I ask you to release me from our engagement, good, kind sir."

"Your sentiments do you credit, dear Miss Witton. But I cannot allow such a sacrifice." He grabbed her hand and pressed his lips to it. "I will make you the woman that you should be—my wife."

She pulled her hand away. "You are too noble, sir. Yours would be the sacrifice, giving up a promising career for the sake of a woman who is losing her senses. I must demand that you release me from my pledge." She levelled a challenging look at him.

Oglesby tapped the papers as he cleared his throat. "Allow me to know what is best for you, dear Miss Witton. A man is wiser in these matters than a frail, weak-minded woman. It is my belief that you have strained your reason with all this needless reading you do. But I leap ahead of myself. That is Item Seven." He cleared his throat again. "Item One: How you shall dress—"

"How I shall dress?" She stared at him, dumbfounded. "Sir! Have you not attended to what I have been saying?"

He allowed himself a condescending smile. "Of course I have, but as yet you have said nothing worth hearing. Now, as to what you will wear as my wife . . . the colours must be subdued. Nothing gives more offence than an overstated style of dress."

"You are jesting, surely?"

He frowned at her. "Naturally you will have to give away those showy gowns you wear. And I will hold all of your jewellery for you until I attain the high office which I seek. My Lord Bishop Oglesby . . ." He breathed deeply, savouring the sound of the words. "With you by my side, I shall no doubt be offered—dare I say it?—Canterbury."

"Mr. Oglesby, pray listen to me. I do not want to be your wife."

"There, there, Miss Witton." He led her toward a chair and pushed her onto it. "This brings me to Item Two—"

She sprang up from the chair, her eyes flashing and chin raised. "You, sir, will have no say in the ordering of my life. For you will be no part of it. I will not marry you!"

His eyes grew larger and his nostrils pinched together. "Item Ten deals with disobedience."

"Blast Item Ten to the devil!" She wrenched Oglesby's token ring off her finger. "Here, take the thing. I don't want it. I don't want *you*. My father shall send a notice to the *Post*. You are free to find yourself another wife. Now go!''

He pursed his lips together in displeasure. "This will not do, Miss Witton. I simply cannot tolerate these outbursts of yours. As for the wedding—why, my uncle, the Bishop of Durham, will have already set out for it. I shall not tolerate its cancellation. You push a man too far."

She glared at him. It appeared that she was not pushing far enough. "I shall call for my father if need be, sir. You do not have to 'tolerate' my decision, merely accept it as a fact. We will not marry."

He stared at her, as if suddenly taking her at her word. His hand clenched his list. "You are a kind-hearted woman to forego your future happiness with me for my sake. But I cannot permit you to do such a thing. Think of the talk there would be."

"I care nothing for what others think of me."

At her words, at her emphatic tone of voice Oglesby's face hardened. His eyes narrowed and, as if dropping a mask, he changed suddenly from fool to malefactor. "You are a heedless, but brave woman," he said icily. "When the world hears that you were seen creeping out of Lord Rossiter's rooms while he was a guest, they will draw their own conclusions. Your reputation will be left in shreds."

"You, sir, are a sneak and tale-bearer. I will have nothing to do with you."

"If you have no consideration for yourself, then think of your esteemed parents, and the shame they will suffer because of your disgrace." He laughed cruelly at her stricken look. "If your mother and father weigh not with you, then think of your sisters."

"My sisters?" Julia could feel herself grow cold as she looked at him.

He smiled like a lizard. "You know how gossip can be. It not only blackens the name of the one involved, but those closest to her. There is no telling what might be said of your sisters."

"What would you say—what would be said, Mr. Oglesby?"

"I daresay that word would spread of Lord Rossiter's tumble in the garden of delights with those very charming Witton sisters. Your home would become known as," he leered, "a house of assignation. You and your sisters would be called ladies of pleasure. It would be said that your mother goes to great lengths to entrap eligible men for her daughters."

"No one of worth would believe such lies!" Julia protested.

"All the world is ready to believe ill of his neighbour. My uncle, the Bishop of Durham, would believe me. And my aunt, who chatters like a magpie, would soon have the tale spread far and wide." He gloated over her stricken look.

"But you have no proof! 'Twould be your word against ours!"

"Yet there is so much to lend credence to the rumours," he continued relentlessly. "Rossiter's hasty flight to London in the middle of the night will be remarked upon. The quick engagement of Miss Marion to the major might be looked upon as a curious event so soon after the departure of a well-known rake and womanizer such as his lordship. If Miss Faith were seen as a plucked flower by some, then we can only decry the harshness of the world and its gossips."

Julia clutched her hands together in dread. "You wouldn't—"

"My dear Miss Witton, as your husband I, of course, would stand by you and your family. But *only* as your husband."

"That is called blackmail, Mr. Oglesby."

"Blackmail is such a disagreeable word." He grinned.

She looked him over distastefully. Could anyone stop him from ruining the reputations of those she held dearest? Could anyone halt this tragedy?

As a woman who fought her own battles, she refused to shrink from the foe before her. If it was a wife he wanted, then, by heaven, a wife he would have. She would save her sisters and sacrifice herself. But by heaven, she would make his life a perpetual Hades, she pledged. And she would never let him touch her.

The murderous look she gave him made him draw back from her. She took the sheaf of papers from his hand. With slow, deliberate movements, she shredded his list before his eyes.

"You shall obey me in all things, Miss Witton." He shuddered at her chuckle as she swept away from him, trailing bits of paper behind her.

Turning, she looked at him frigidly. "It is said, Mr. Oglesby, that women are like wasps in their anger. Pray you remember that in future." She was about to withdraw when her father entered the room.

"Bishop Witton!" Oglesby exclaimed, bowing. "How kind of you to join us."

The bishop ignored the rector, going straight to his daughter. "I was told you wished to speak to me, my dear."

"Ah, yes," Oglesby inserted. He moved to stand beside Julia. "She wished to discuss some changes in our nuptials." He cleared his throat. "It is her sincere desire to be wed as soon as possible. She has no wish for the trappings of a large wedding and the waiting has had an adverse effect upon her nerves. Her fondest wish is to be married by tomorrow evening. I, of course, am willing to comply."

"Is this your wish, daughter?"

Julia shook with suppressed fury. But mutely she nodded her head.

Oglesby placed a hand on her shoulder until the savage look she gave him caused him to ease away from her. "Our pledge to each other is quite binding, milord," he said. "I would rather die than crush the expectations of my dearest love."

His dearest raised her brows in a speculative fashion at the notion of his death. She shrugged off the pleasing prospect after giving it some thought.

"Are you quite sure *you* want this wedding, my dear?" the bishop asked.

She stared at Oglesby. His placid face did not disguise the warning in his eyes. He would do his worst if she refused. "I will marry him," she stated numbly.

"Very well, then there is much to attend to before tomorrow evening." The bishop eyed the rector but said nothing.

JULIA HELD HERSELF in taut control. She scarcely noticed when her mother left her side. The cathedral, though almost bare of well-wishers, soon filled with music coming from the loft above. To Julia, the selection sounded morose and mocking.

"I never thought you would be so mutton-headed as to go through with this insanity," Sarah whispered, as she and her sisters gathered around Julia.

For their sakes, Julia held to her determination. Even when Faith began to cry, Julia would not be moved from her course. She kept her eyes directed straight ahead.

The music began to swell, signalling the start of the wedding procession.

"Goosecap!" Sarah looked at Julia before walking up the aisle.

"Why, Julia? You never used to be so brainless," Marion offered, then followed Sarah.

"Oooh..." Faith cried, dropping tear after tear as she joined the procession.

The music reached the height of its volume, indicating that Julia was to begin walking up the centre aisle of the nave. She remained where she stood. After a time the music stopped. Everyone paused to look back at her. She jerked her head in a nod, a cue for the procession to continue. A musician rapped his bow upon a stand and the music began again.

Julia forced herself to take the first step and follow it with another. She looked up at the scissor arch. It blurred before her until she blinked it back into focus. Her steps dragged as she lifted one foot, then the other, making her way through the choir. Finally she was standing before the High Altar, her gaze fixed upon her father.

"Dearly beloved," the bishop began, "we are gathered together in the sight of God..."

As her father continued to read the preliminary words of the ceremony, his voice became a dull echo in Julia's mind. She stared ahead, unseeing. Thomas's name, his voice, his image, circled in her thoughts. She could not dispel him from her being. He was too much a part of her. How she wanted him, to be reassured again by his smile. She wanted his arms about her, holding her tight until her bones ached.

Her father's words broke in upon her thoughts. "Therefore if any man can show any just cause why they may not lawfully be joined together, let him speak now; or else hereafter forever hold his peace." The bishop looked around at the small company assembled. There was a general murmur, but no one spoke up.

Raising his book, the bishop continued to read. "I require and charge you, as you will answer at the dreadful Day of Judgment, when the secrets of all hearts shall be disclosed, that if either of you do know any impediment why ye may not be lawfully joined together in Matrimony, that ye confess it . . ."

Julia swallowed the words that pushed to get out. She closed her eyes to the intense look her father gave her. Yet, from deep within, she was impelled to be honest. Little by little she began to shake her head until she was vehemently denying any desire to continue. "Father, I cannot!"

Oglesby grabbed her arm. "Remember your sisters," he hissed. "They will never marry if it is believed that Rossiter has been with them." His voice carried to her ears alone, as he smiled at the bishop and crushed her arm in a vicious grasp.

She groaned and pulled away from him. Gathering the train of her gown, she hastened down the aisle.

Oglesby spluttered and gasped, then rushed after her. He was followed close behind by the rest of the wedding party.

At one of the columns supporting the central arch, Julia turned to confront her bridegroom, firm in her resolve. His furious demeanour could not intimidate her.

"How dare you!" The rector looked ready to smite her.

From the empty nave came the sound of spurred boots striking the stone floor. Oglesby looked for the source of the interruption, then he fell back a step, his eyes bulging with fear, his face drained of colour. The rapid heaving of his chest matched the rhythm of the advancing boots.

"Thomas," Julia said softly. She smiled in such a way that it was a salute of love witnessed by all.

Rossiter, in dirt-encrusted boots and with a day's growth of beard upon his face, came to her as if nothing would dare get in his way. He stopped a few paces before her and held out his hand. The patch seemed to wink at her.

She went to him slowly, savouring his gaze upon her. She put her hand in his, saying, "I love you, Thomas."

Without a thought to who might be watching, Rossiter took her in his arms and thoroughly demonstrated his feeling for her with a powerful kiss, which lasted much too long to be considered proper.

Faced with the sight of the embracing couple, and spying the look of fury the bishop cast him, Oglesby did the only manly thing left to him. He fainted.

CHAPTER EIGHTEEN

"MR. OGLESBY!" The bishop's wife knelt beside the fallen rector. She took out her vinaigrette and thrust it under his nose. One of Oglesby's eyes popped open, then closed as a press of people bent over him.

When at last Julia and Thomas pulled apart, Julia gave her betrothed a questioning look before drawing Rossiter aside. "How did you know to come?" she asked.

"Your father sent for me." He glanced about, then took in her gown. "What is this nonsense about a wedding?"

Julia's words were few as she explained what had passed between Oglesby and herself, but the effect of those words was immediate.

With brows drawn together and jaw clenched tight, Thomas turned and strode over to the seemingly unconscious rector.

"A bit of air is what the fellow needs." So saying, Thomas grabbed Oglesby by the lapels and heaved him over his shoulder, then marched down the aisle to the west doors.

"Oooh..." Oglesby groaned, and his eyes flew open. His entreaties for deliverance went unanswered.

Julia held her mother back, allowing Thomas the pleasure of dispatching the rector. In a voice so low that even her sisters standing nearby could not hear, she explained to her parents how Oglesby had got her to continue with the engagement.

The bishop looked grim. "I wish you had come to me, Julia. I'd have dealt with the vermin."

"He would have denied it, yet it was a threat that I knew would be carried out. The man is beneath contempt—a thorough swine."

"Are you speaking of Mr. Oglesby?" Sarah asked as she joined them. She turned to her sister. "Julia, I never knew you loved Lord Rossiter. All this time you've been playing fast and loose with that pasty-faced rector and you'd given your heart to another. I call that wonderful!"

"Sarah . . ." the Bishop warned.

"The child brings to mind an important point," Amanda said, staring at Julia. "What is this attachment between you and Lord Rossiter?"

Julia looked down at her hands. "I am quite sure of my feelings for him, but he has yet to declare himself."

"The man's smitten," Amanda stated. "Anyone can see that. How odd I did not realize it before."

"Mama, I hope what you say is true." Julia watched Thomas stride purposefully toward her.

Lord Rossiter bowed before the bishop and said, "I shall of course call upon you formally tomorrow, my lord, but for now, may I be granted permission to address your eldest daughter?"

"But what of Oglesby?" the bishop asked.

"I have taken care of him." Thomas looked as if he would say no more.

Amanda appeared to want further enlightenment. "Oh?"

"I informed Mr. Oglesby," Thomas said quietly, "that if any rumours concerning the Witton family were tossed about I should consider it a personal insult. And I would shoot the perpetrator down in the street like a rabid dog.''

The bishop suppressed a smile. "Worthy sentiments, sir. I pray you will never have cause to execute your promise. A forced exile for my daughter and her husband would displease me excessively." He looked from Julia to Rossiter. "You will wish to talk in private, I daresay.''

"But, my dear bishop," Amanda protested faintly, "this cannot be. Think what will be said. Julia has jilted a man at the altar. Granted, she had good cause, but the particulars must never be known. A hurried marriage to another, now, will only precipitate a scandal I shudder to even consider.''

"We shall contrive to scrape through somehow, my dear," the bishop assured her.

"Then I insist," Amanda declared, "that his lordship at least, ah, restrain from enjoying his conjugal rights. There must be a proper lapse of time between the wedding and the birth of the first child.''

Sarah's eyes grew rounded. "Oh! Is *that* what conjugal rights mean?" Her mother reddened and ordered Sarah back to the carriage. The girl shuffled down the aisle.

"Well?" Amanda turned to look at the couple inquiringly. "Will you promise?''

"Mama," Julia said, "a man is bound to get a bit out of sorts if denied his honeymoon." She smiled at Thomas and, despite his best efforts to suppress it, he smiled back. He caught her hand and led her out a side door and along the cloister to the garden by the moat. As he halted, she ran laughing headlong into his arms. She gazed at him, mischief dancing in her eyes.

"I've a mind to have your father draw up a special licence," Thomas said. "I'll not have a known jilt balk at the last moment with me." He chuckled. "You shall have to mend your wicked ways if you are to be my wife."

She leaned back in his arms and tilted her head in a considering fashion. "Am I to be your wife? How odd. I do not recall being asked."

He looked at her quite seriously. "I love you. Will you marry me, Julia Witton?"

"Yes, Thomas, I will."

"Will you marry me in a month's time? I vow I'll not wait a moment longer to have you."

She ran her finger along his cheek. "I'll marry you within the month—in a fortnight if you like."

He threw back his head and laughed, an exultant sound that rose to the spires of the cathedral. "A fortnight it shall be, and the devil take the consequences!" He gathered her to him. "I've reconsidered. Do not mend your wicked ways. They are much too delightful." He kissed her, slowly and thoroughly.

As their lips parted she began to caress his chin, teasing his mouth with the tip of her finger. Then she trailed it up his cheek to the silver patch. "There is one small thing that I would have you do. I fear, Thomas, that your roving days as a spy must end. It is time to come out from behind the patch, don't you think?"

"I question whether Society is ready for such a revelation."

"It will probably be said that, for a glass one, your eye looks quite genuine."

His brows drew together. "I do not have a glass eye. Both are quite genuine, as you say."

She lifted the patch and sighed. "'Tis a pity to hide such a handsome eye."

He removed the patch and held it by the string. He looked at the bit of silver swinging back and forth, then at Julia. "Only for you. I shall do it only for you." Thomas tossed the patch over his shoulder, where it plopped into the water of the moat.

"'And the devil take the consequences.'" She smiled at him as she quoted his own words.

They wandered away from the moat and into the cathedral. Using a series of side doors, they ended at the west front. He put his arm about her waist and she leaned her head upon his shoulder as they strolled out to the green.

Thomas looked down at her. "You shall have to keep me occupied if I am to give up my work for the Crown. Ah, yes ... those delightful conjugal rights." His lips gently devoured hers in a kiss that claimed her—body, mind and soul.

SARAH WATCHED in fascination from across the grounds. The rest of the Witton family came out of the west doors, now bathed in the golden light of the setting sun, and began to enter the carriages.

"Sarah, do stop hanging out the window," Amanda admonished. "Who are you gawking at?"

"Lord Rossiter and Julia. Mama, he's not wearing his patch."

Amanda moaned and fanned herself.

"I wonder if his eye is glass." Sarah kept peering out the window. "Perhaps he'll take it out and show it to me."

With a hand over her heart, Amanda gasped, "I sincerely hope not." She pulled Sarah back. "Cease your gawking at Julia and his lordship. It is most improper to stare at someone with an affliction."

As the carriage moved away, Sarah craned her head to look at the entwined couple. If that was what it was like to be afflicted, then she could hardly wait to be so herself.

Harlequin Regency Romance™

COMING NEXT MONTH

#5 COUSIN NANCY by Alberta Sinclair
Nancy Browne is a penniless orphan, but everyone loves her for her natural country charm and spontaneous good humour. When she arrives at the country estate of her cousins, she is introduced to their neighbour, the Earl of Selbridge. She is promptly smitten but fears a match impossible, being poor and without position. Little does she know this matters not to the Earl, who returns her affection secretly. To win the Earl she must prove herself to be a proper lady. She does not reckon on his perplexing reaction.

#6 FALSE IMPRESSIONS by Margaret Westhaven
Being twenty and nine, Theodora Thornfield decides to accept a position as paid companion to her cousin and go to London. She does not expect to attract any suitors, but Mr. Lawrence Carruthers, a handsome, wealthy landowner, wastes no time in bespeaking his interest in her. Dora is flattered until she learns that Mr. Carruthers means to make her his next mistress. Dora owns that she may be "on the shelf," but never would she be that desperate!

ANNOUNCING . . .

The Lost Moon Flower
by Bethany Campbell

Look for it this August
wherever Harlequins are sold

HR 3000-1